CELESTE FILES:
PRIMAL

BY
KRISTINE MASON

Copyright © 2017 Kristine Thompson

All rights reserved. Except for use in any review, the reproduction or utilization of this work in whole or in part in any form by any electronic, mechanical or other means, now known or hereafter invented, including xerography, photocopying and recording, or in any information storage or retrieval system, is forbidden without the written permission of the author.

This is a work of fiction. Names, characters, places and incidents are either the product of the author's imagination or are used fictitiously, and any resemblance to actual persons, living or dead, business establishments, events or locales is entirely coincidental.

Print Edition

ISBN 13: 978-0-9977831-5-5
ISBN10: 0-9977831-5-X

Dedication

For Celeste…

You're not real, but writing about you reminds me to stay strong and confident, and to take risks. That being said, I'm sorry for what I'm about to do to you.

Acknowledgements

Special thanks to my critique partner and friend, Jamie Denton, for helping me with this book and believing in this series. I'd also like to thank my editor, Tessa Shapcott, my proofreader, Sherry Fundin, and my cover artist, Elle J Rossi of EJR Digital Arts. This cover is fierce!

CHAPTER 1

Thirty-five years ago...
The Ryker Residence, Silver Spring, Maryland
Saturday, 3:34 p.m. Eastern Daylight Time

EVERY NERVE ENDING in my body burst to life. I bit down on the plastic mouth guard. Fought the agony, the helplessness, the fear of the unknown. My body, stiff and moving on its own, convulsed against the restraints around my shoulders, waist and legs. Pain shot through my skull, pierced my brain, stimulated the muscles in my face and made my heart beat erratically. Panicking, I cried out, but my screams of terror were muffled by the mouth guard and the loud humming of the machine connected to my head.

"Relax, Karen," Dr. Ryker said as he removed the electrodes from my temple.

Nurse Martha smiled as she used her body to keep mine from jerking. "Yes, you're doing just fine."

I wasn't fine. After having gone through electroshock therapy more times than I could remember, I didn't think I'd ever be fine again. Breathing hard, spit filled my dry mouth, while my stomach rolled with nausea and my throat tightened with the urge to vomit. Tears filled my eyes. I swallowed back the rising acid and used my tongue to push against the mouth guard until it fell from my lips.

When a gasp came from the doorway, I turned my head and blinked back the tears until my vision sharpened and my gaze locked on a boy with blue eyes and light brown hair. I knew Dr.

Ryker had a son and had overheard him say something about the kid to the nurse. I also knew his name, but couldn't remember it right now. I couldn't remember how I even came to be in this place.

"You're not supposed to be here," Dr. Ryker said to the boy.

As my limbs continued to twitch, Nurse Martha unhooked the restraint around my waist, only to make it tighter. "Oh, Seth, let him stay."

"He's too young."

"I'm ten," the boy said, straightening his bony shoulders and pushing out his thin chest. He knocked his bangs from his forehead and stared at her. "Is she the one who's like Jean Grey?"

"Who?" Dr. Ryker asked.

"Jean Grey. She's a human mutant from *X-Men* and has telepathic and telekinetic powers."

Now I remembered how I ended up here. After our church minister had ruled out demonic possession, he'd recommended that my parents take me to see Dr. Ryker. According to our minister, the psychiatrist had been known to cure people like me. *Human mutants* who could do unexplainable things with their minds. But I'm not a mutant. I'm a seventeen-year-old girl who happens to have a weird, yet special gift.

Nurse Martha chuckled. "Human mutant," she repeated, and looked to Dr. Ryker. "That sounds accurate, no?"

The doctor didn't crack a smile. Ignoring Martha, he glanced to the boy. "Aiden, son, there are no such things as mutants."

"Well, she sure looks like one. I ain't never seen anyone who looks like her."

How many times had I been stared at and ridiculed? I hadn't asked to be born without pigment, and I was certain my parents hadn't prayed for an albino baby who looked as if she'd been dipped in flour.

"*Have never*," Martha corrected the kid.

The boy rolled his eyes at the nurse and refocused on his father. "Every person you bring to this house has a power. The lady in the attic who can predict the future? She's like Destiny."

"And is Destiny also from *X-Men*?"

The kid nodded. "But she's a nemesis. Then there's the guy in our basement. He's kinda like Cyclops."

Dr. Ryker frowned. "The man who can shoot lasers from his eyes?"

"Yeah," the boy said, smiling.

"Aiden, that is physically impossible. My patient cannot do any such thing."

"Then why do you and Grandma wear safety suits when you go into his room?"

"Why are you spying on us?" Dr. Ryker countered. "My equipment is very expensive, and some of it is dangerous." He approached his son and placed a hand on the boy's shoulder. "My work is very important. I know you're curious about what I'm doing here, but you're just too young to fully comprehend it."

Aiden's blue eyes widened. "You're like Weapon X."

"Who is?"

"Not a who, but a super-secret government agency that does genetic experiments on mutants."

"The child has your imagination," Nurse Martha said. "Don't stifle it. After all, your wild ideas led you to become a psychiatrist, and look at all the good work you've done for your patients, and even the government."

"The government?" Aiden echoed with awe.

"It's not what you think." Dr. Ryker returned to the bed, then began examining my eyes with a light. "I've assisted the FBI by creating psychiatric assessments for the criminals they're trying to capture. Nothing more. My colleagues at the FBI aren't aware of my research in parapsychology. And other branches of the government aren't interested in my work. It's not considered mainstream science, after all."

"But I bet if your experiments work, they'll give you a job." The boy's eyes glittered with excitement. "Or maybe the President will."

Dr. Ryker's face became blotchy and red. He turned to his son and gripped his shoulders. "No one can know about these experiments. Understand? Have you told anyone about my patients?"

"Mutants are cool. When I grow up, I'm going to experiment on them, too."

The doctor gave his son a slight shake. "Stop and look at me. Focus on my words. This is a very big secret. No one can know. Now answer me. Have you told anyone?"

"No, sir."

"Don't lie to me. Because I have a machine that will force the truth from you."

"Hook me up to it," Aiden challenged. "I haven't told anyone. I swear."

Dr. Ryker ruffled Aiden's hair. "You're a good kid. Now go back upstairs. Grandma will join you soon to start dinner."

As the boy left the room, a dull throb began to develop in my temple, just as it had the last three times Dr. Ryker had given me electroshock therapy. I ignored the pain and instead repeated in my head everything I'd just witnessed. With each treatment, my memory lapsed and I wanted to retain what I'd heard. Nurse Martha was clearly the boy's grandmother, so I assumed she was the doctor's mother. The dynamic was strange, but what was even stranger and scarier was that there were other people here. And no one was supposed to know Dr. Ryker was experimenting on them.

Fear crawled along my skin. Did my parents know what was happening? Were the families of the others aware? And where was I? Aiden had mentioned an attic and basement, and Grandma was going to be heading upstairs soon to make dinner, so could this be Dr. Ryker's house? If it was, I couldn't believe my parents would allow this man to keep me under his roof for... How many days had I been here?

"When are my mom and dad coming to see me?" I asked, panicking.

Dr. Ryker pressed a stethoscope against my chest. After a moment, he settled his gaze on mine. "Can you hear my thoughts?"

"I don't know. I didn't try."

"Give it a shot," he suggested with an easy smile. "I'm thinking about my answer. Ready?"

I held his gaze and nodded. Concentrated on my breathing, on his, until I heard a faint whisper. One word, repeated over and over.

Never.

Present day...
Maxine Morehouse's Residence, Chicago, Illinois
Friday, 11:05 a.m. Central Daylight Time

TENSION WORKED ITS way into Celeste Kain's shoulders and neck. She opened her eyes and met Maxine's gaze. "Sorry, I'm just not feeling it today," she said, letting out a deep breath. Although she'd already performed one psychic exercise this morning, she and her mentor had wanted to work more on her ability to shift her spirit from her own body—something she'd accidentally done in the past, then again purposefully a couple months ago. Except she hadn't been able to replicate that part of her gift since. After nearly losing her husband, she'd been so down, she hadn't had the energy to do much of anything.

"No worries, dear." Maxine leaned into the wingback chair upholstered with unicorn-patterned fabric, just one of the many eclectic items in what her friend called the Unicorn Parlor. "You've been so stressed lately, I honestly didn't expect our exercise to work today." She studied Celeste with both curiosity and concern. "You're supposed to be looking forward to a vacation, not dreading it."

"I don't know where that came from, but I never said I was *dreading* our vacation," Celeste replied, then glanced to the portable infant carrier seat holding her six-month-old son, Mason. The little chub was becoming too big to carry around, but he'd fallen asleep during the drive to Maxine's, and she was a firm believer in never waking a sleeping baby. When Mason yawned and opened his eyes, she immediately relaxed. Like her daughter, Olivia, and her husband, John, one look from Mason could calm her and remind her life was good. Even if there were times when her world was filled with dark chaos and…fear.

"No, but you haven't acted excited about making the trip home. You're leaving today and haven't said a word about it."

Celeste bent down and unhooked Mason from the carrier. "I was at first, but now…not so much." She lifted Mason into her arms, then seated him on her lap so he faced forward. "I wanted to go home, see friends and neighbors, check out the diner my family used to own and show John the fun side of Wissota Falls, Wisconsin. But instead of thinking about picnicking, fishing trips, or sightseeing, I keep focusing on my mother," she said, heaviness settling on her chest.

Her mom had been gone for over six years, and the loss still hurt. When she'd originally told John that she wanted to head to Wissota Falls for their family vacation, she had been going through a rough period. At that time, her husband had just been released from the hospital, her confidence had been shaken from being unable to combat the evil spirit who'd been tormenting him and tearing apart their family, and she'd started to doubt her psychic ability as a gift. Needing an escape from her reality, she'd had the overwhelming urge to go *home*. To surround herself with childhood memories, and take herself back to a time when she was simply the goofy kid who could dream about missing jewelry or animals, then wake up and find them. To a time when the dead had left her alone.

"I wouldn't expect any less." Maxine picked up a stuffed toy shaped like a unicorn and made a silly face at Mason. "You miss her, yet you harbor bitterness toward her."

Celeste stiffened. Even her son's giggles couldn't calm her agitation. "I absolutely *do not* feel any bitterness."

Maxine cocked a silver brow. "My apologies," she said, reaching for Mason.

Celeste let her take the baby, then crossed her arms over her chest. She wasn't bitter, she was sad and angry. Sad her mom was gone, and angry because her mom had kept so many secrets from her, secrets that could have possibly made life as a clairvoyant medium easier.

"Don't apologize. I'm in a sensitive mood. I mean, what was I thinking? John suggested we vacation at a beach resort and, instead, I come up with the brilliant idea of dragging my family to Wisconsin."

"If you don't want to go, tell John you changed your mind," Maxine suggested, as a string of drool oozed from Mason's mouth and onto her pants. "No one said you had to do this."

Celeste leaned forward and used a dry bib to wipe Mason's face. "I know, but I already paid for the place we're renting. Although…the owners did call last night and told us we couldn't get into it until tomorrow. The air conditioning tanked and they're having it fixed."

"But you're still planning on leaving today?"

Celeste shrugged. "Everything's packed, so we figured we'd drive for a few hours, then stay at a hotel. In the morning, after breakfast, we'll head to Irvine Park Zoo and hang out there until our rental is ready."

"I loathe the zoo," Maxine said, wrinkling her nose.

"So do I, but Olivia will love it." Celeste gave Maxine the bib, which Mason fisted and immediately tried to put in his mouth. "It'll be fine. The trip will be nice."

Maxine grinned. "Are you trying to convince me, or yourself?"

Celeste sighed. "I haven't been back home since I moved to Chicago. And just before I moved, I was kidnapped and nearly killed. I hadn't given what had happened to me much thought over the years, because the men John stopped weren't worth my energy. Except ever since I booked the rental, I *have* been thinking about them, about the women they killed, about how much my gift had awakened during the murder investigation."

"Perhaps you're also thinking about how you ended up suppressing your gift shortly thereafter. Are you worried it might happen again?"

Celeste shook her head. "I'm too aware now. Being psychic is such a part of me, I can't see that ever changing again. My gut tells me my gift will only get stronger, and that worries me. As it is, I don't always know how to handle the abilities I already have."

"Which brings us full circle," Maxine said, dodging Mason's chubby fingers before he could yank out her hoop earrings.

"You mean, this brings us back to my mom and what she never bothered to tell me," Celeste replied with a nod. "What's interesting is that I've read all the journals she left behind, and there isn't much there that could help me. But I do feel like I'm missing some of them. Over the years, she wrote in her journal a few times a month. Yet there are gaps between some of the earlier diaries. I'm talking six months to a year."

"Maybe she was too busy to write," Maxine suggested.

"I suppose it doesn't matter, since I'll never know."

A cold draft filled the room. Mason stopped grabbing for Maxine's earrings and tried to twist his little body to face forward. A chill ran up Celeste's spine as she followed her son's dark gaze to the parlor door. Edward, Maxine's great-great uncle and self-proclaimed head house-ghost, hovered at the entrance. Edward was pompous, but sweet. He didn't scare Celeste, nor did the other ghosts who resided under Maxine's roof. What bothered her was that Mason—at six months old—could sense when the dead were among them. If he could do this now, what would he be capable of five years from now?

"Hello, Edward," Celeste greeted the spirit.

"Good day, Celeste. Young Mason is looking quite healthy. How does Olivia fare? It's been far too long since we've seen the little miss."

Other than the occasional swim in Maxine's pool, Celeste had made a point of not bringing Olivia inside this house. The last time she had, Celeste had caught her daughter rolling a ball back and forth with one of the ghosts, while several others had smiled on with delight. Although Celeste knew her daughter had her gift, like Mason, Olivia was too young to understand the difference between the dead and the living. And Celeste wanted her kids' childhoods to be as normal as possible.

"Liv is doing great. I'm sure she would love to see you, too, but she's having a play date at my sister's."

"Do be a dear and bring her around again. No offense to my niece, but we miss the youthful laughter of children. Oh, how it warms the soul," Edward said with a genuine smile.

"What does my darling uncle want?" Maxine asked. Though Maxine was also psychic, her gift was different from Celeste's. Maxine could read peoples' pasts and feel their emotions through touch, but she couldn't see ghosts. Which was probably a good thing, otherwise she and Edward would constantly bicker. As it was, Maxine and Edward weren't getting along right now. Edward had accused Maxine's last boyfriend, Diego, of being in *cahoots* with her housekeeper, Alison. He'd been convinced Diego was using Maxine and, like Alison, stealing from her.

Edward cleared his throat. *"Please inform my niece that the maid has stolen money from the bedroom dresser. Again."*

After Celeste repeated what Edward said, Maxine frowned. "Oh, really? Just as Diego stole my diamond bracelet?"

Edward's spirit reddened before returning to normal. *"I apologized for accusing Diego and thus causing the two of you to end your arrangement. I hadn't realized the jewelry had fallen into the wrong drawer."*

Celeste relayed the message. Rather than accept Edward's apology, Maxine handed Mason to Celeste, then stood. "Instead of giving me the opportunity to look for the damned thing, you scared the bejesus out of my Spanish lover. The man ran from my house in only his underwear!"

Celeste pressed her lips together to keep from laughing, while Edward turned red again.

"He was beneath you anyway," Edward argued.

Maxine held up a hand. "Don't bother repeating anything else he has to say. I'm sure I'll get over this invasion of privacy, but until then, I want Edward to mind his own business."

Edward's spirit became gray as hurt and confusion crossed his face. *"Celeste, please ask my niece, at the very least, to question the maid. The chit has a one hundred dollar bill in the left back pocket of her pants."*

"Maxine," Celeste began, "how much do you pay Alison?"

"It depends. Today, she'll be here for four hours, so I'll pay her one hundred dollars. Why? Do you believe Edward?"

As Mason gnawed on his hand, creating spit bubbles with his drool, Celeste nodded and reached for the bib. "He feels bad about Diego."

"I most certainly do not." Edward straightened. *"Maxine can do much better than that leech."*

"And," Celeste continued, ignoring the ghost, "he claims Alison has a one hundred dollar bill in her back left pocket."

"Even if she does, how do I know she stole it from me? What proof is there?" Maxine asked.

"Inform my stubborn niece that this particular bill has a purple line down the middle."

Celeste set Mason in his carrier and began buckling the straps. "Edward, all the new bills have that. Do you know what the serial number is on the bill?"

Emma, a young female ghost, who Celeste had recently learned was Edward's daughter-in-law, appeared in the room. *"I know the numbers,"* she said, then, once Celeste had pen and paper, she gave them to Celeste.

As Celeste wrote the last number, Maxine's housekeeper, Alison, knocked on the opened door. "Ms. Morehouse, I'm finished for today." She smiled at Mason, then explained what rooms she'd cleaned, and to what extent.

"Excellent. Thank you, Alison." Maxine shifted her gaze to Celeste. "I…ah…" She cleared her throat and focused on the housekeeper. "This might sound like a strange question, but do you have a one hundred dollar bill in your back left pocket?"

Alison's cheeks turned pink. "I do. After I started cleaning here, I realized I'd worn these pants yesterday, but forgot to take out the money my other employer paid me."

"Interesting." Maxine folded her hands on her lap. "Because I just so happen to be missing a bill from my drawer. Mind pulling it out and giving me the serial number?"

Alison's brows drew together. "Are you accusing me of *stealing?*"

"I am. The serial number, please."

When the woman crossed her arms and glared at Maxine, Edward rose toward the ceiling. Seconds later, the crystal chandelier swayed. As the glass pieces jingled, Emma slid one of the many unicorn figurines Maxine had collected over the years across the credenza she used as an informal bar.

Alison dropped her arms, shifted her gaze from the ceiling to the credenza and took a jerky backward step. "It's my money."

"My ghosts say otherwise." Maxine glanced to the swaying chandelier and smiled. "But give me the serial number and prove them wrong." When Edward moved to the drapes and caused them to billow, she added, "Hurry. They're growing impatient and angry. As am I."

With tears in her eyes, the housekeeper pulled the bill from her back pocket. Her hand trembled as she set the money on the credenza. "I'm so sorry, Ms. Morehouse. Please don't call the police."

Maxine held up a hand. "You also took my mother's ring. I want it back."

"She pilfered your ex-husband's Rolex watch, too," Edward said. *"Husband number three's, I believe."*

Celeste quickly relayed the message to Maxine, who simply shook her head. "I want the watch back, along with anything else you've taken from me."

"There was nothing else, I swear." Alison hugged herself. "I pawned the watch, but I still have the ring. I...I can't afford to get the watch back." A tear slipped down her cheek. "My eleven-year-old son has Hodgkin's lymphoma. My husband lost his job back in the spring when the company he worked for sold the business. We lost our health insurance and have been struggling to pay for coverage out of our own pockets. My husband just started a new job last week, but we're still so far behind on our finances." She wiped her cheeks. "Please don't call the police. I'll work for free to pay for the watch."

"I'm sorry to hear about your son. Still, stealing isn't the answer." Maxine nodded to the credenza. "Take the money, that's what I would've paid you anyway. And I expect you to return my mother's ring. I'm sure the pawnbroker told you it was worthless, but it means something to me."

"What about the watch?" Alison asked.

Maxine shrugged. "I honestly forgot I still had it. And I'm going to forget you stole it. Now, take the money and leave," she said, then escorted the woman out of the room.

If Alison was being honest, Celeste's heart went out to her and her family. The woman's tragic story also reminded her that she should appreciate how good her life was, rather than dwelling on the negative.

She gathered up her purse and diaper bag. Her arm muscles strained when she lifted the carrier. "You're getting too big to lug around like this," she informed Mason as she also left the room. She met Maxine in the foyer, which was, with the exception of Edward, now empty. "Do you think Alison was telling the truth about her son?"

"One hundred percent," Maxine said with sadness in her tone and eyes. "I touched her and not only saw what her family has been dealing with, but I felt her pain and anxiety about her son and financial issues. When she returns with the ring, I'm going to tell her she can keep her job if she still wants it. I sensed stealing is extremely out of character for her."

"You're a good person." Celeste set the carrier on the wood floor to give her mentor a hug. "I have to go pick up Olivia. I'll call or text while we're out of town."

"Be safe." Maxine bent down to smooth her hand over Mason's dark hair. "Take care of your mommy," she said, standing. "Celeste, before you go, could you please tell Edward I'm sorry. I should have listened to him from the start."

Celeste grinned when Edward's spirit took on a lovely shade of lavender. "You just did. He's standing right next to you."

"And will you please tell my niece I accept her apologies."

Once Celeste did, Maxine let out a breath. "I'm relieved the family feud has come to an end. I have a date this evening and I don't want my darling uncle, or his ghostly cohorts to scare him away."

"Oh, dear. Another suitor?"

Celeste hid a smile and, to keep the peace, chose to not tell Maxine what Edward had said. "Would this date be with the history professor?" Celeste asked. After Maxine's recent breakup with Diego, her mentor had met Dr. Charles Warren while at a coffee shop. Since then they'd gone on several dates. Though Celeste hadn't met the man yet, it was clear Maxine was falling for him. And if Maxine was happy, that made Celeste happy, too. Besides, after seven failed marriages, Maxine was bound to eventually find the right man for her. No one could be that unlucky in love.

Maxine blushed. "Yes. Charles is taking me to dinner, then I thought we would come back here. After all, my house is steeped in history."

"Quite true. Especially my dear niece's bedroom."

Celeste glared at Edward who, with a chuckle, quickly faded away. "Well, I hope you two have a nice time. Send me a text and let me know how things go."

When she hugged her friend again, Maxine squeezed her tightly. "And I hope you find whatever it is you're looking for during your journey."

Celeste pulled away and hefted the carrier. "I'm not looking for anything but relaxation."

Maxine cocked a brow. "And maybe a few ghosts to guide you?" She gave Celeste a soft smile and touched her shoulder.

"Your grandmother, great-grandmother and mom all died in the same small town. Aren't you the least bit curious to see if you can contact them?"

"I haven't given it any thought," Celeste replied, then added, "My arm is going to fall off from lugging Goo Goo Goliath. I need to get going."

Maxine gave her a tolerant smile. "I love chubby babies, and you're a terrible liar."

Celeste rolled her eyes. "Okay, so maybe I thought about reaching out to my mom and grandmothers. Let's face it, though, the chances of making a connection are slim. Ghosts come to me, not the other way around."

"This is true. But if you do make a connection, please be careful."

"We're talking about my mom and grandmas. All of them loved me."

"Of that I have no doubt. I'm more concerned with what they might reveal. Perhaps there's a reason your mother kept secrets from you. Maybe she didn't want you to follow in her footsteps. Her work with the FBI was very dangerous and almost got her killed."

Celeste opened the front door. "Dangerous? I own a bakery and yet I've been attacked, possessed and almost died. I know I don't even need to get into what's happened to my husband." She shook her head. "No. What's dangerous is having a powerful gift and not knowing how to use it."

And she was determined to find out exactly how much power she possessed.

CHAPTER 2

Fairmont Inn, Madison, Wisconsin
Friday, 6:19 p.m. Central Daylight Time

JOHN KAIN FINISHED sending an email to Hudson, his brother-in-law and fellow CORE agent, then set his phone inside one of the center console's empty cup holders. He glanced toward the hotel lobby, then turned in the driver's seat and smiled at Mason. "Feeling better, buddy?" Poor kid had been crying for the past thirty minutes. Prior to that, he'd vomited twice. Nothing like a road trip to help you discover your kid has motion sickness. While Mason no longer cried, his round cheeks were still red from the exertion, and the front of his onesie was soaked with drool.

"He can't talk," Olivia, Master of the Obvious, reminded him.

"I know that. Daddy was just a little worried about our guy."

"Mommy mad."

"No, she's not." John glanced toward the glass doors of the hotel lobby. "Maybe a little." Probably a lot. The original plan was to drive until they reached Black River Falls, which was only an hour outside of Wissota Falls, their final destination. Between the vomiting and crying, he and Celeste had decided pushing to drive an additional two hours wasn't worth the headache, and that they'd better call it a night here in Madison. "Are you excited about staying in a hotel room?"

Liv clapped, while Mason grabbed his toes. "We go swim!"

"That's right. We'll swim, then how about we get pizza for dinner?"

His daughter furrowed her forehead and looked at him as if he were in an idiot. "Mason no eat pizza. He a baby."

John laughed. "Right you are." He glanced out the passenger window as Celeste held open the hotel's glass door for an elderly woman. "All set?" he asked, once his wife was inside the van.

"Yep. Except the only rooms available have single, king-sized beds. We'll use the portable crib for Mason, and Olivia will have to sleep with us."

While Olivia clapped again, John didn't bother to complain. Hotel sex was awesome, but not with two kids in the room. "I'll set up the crib and go get the pizza, while you take the kids to the pool." When Celeste leveled him with the same puzzled look Olivia had given him seconds ago, and he thought about how much of a hassle it would be to take a three-year-old and six-month-old to a pool—alone—he shook his head. "Never mind. That was *not* a good plan."

"Yeah, not really." Celeste put on her seatbelt. "Our room is on the third floor on the far side of the building," she said, pointing ahead. "We can park there, or would it be easier if I get a luggage cart and go through the lobby?"

It amazed John how many things two small children required. Between the portable crib, the stroller, diaper bag, overnight bag, favorite blankets and toys, bottles and baby food, it would take him three trips to haul everything to the room without using a cart. He leaned closer to Celeste, unbuckled her seatbelt and gave her a kiss. "I'll help you and the kids to the room, and while you three relax, I'll bring everything up there."

Offering to take care of their things while she and the kids hung out in the room didn't erase the stress etched on his wife's face. He knew preparing for the trip had been hard on Celeste. Prior to leaving, she'd had meetings with her managers who helped run her bakery, had dealt with business suppliers, made arrangements for the dog, packed and had taken care of other odds and ends like catching up on bills and stopping the mail. For nearly a week, she'd been anxious and short tempered. He'd helped her where he could, yet that had done little to ease the tension. And when he'd asked her what was wrong, she had given him the vague answer, 'Nothing'. Of course he hadn't believed her, and suspected her mood stemmed from not only what had happened to him last month, but also because she was going home for the first time in years. While part of him understood her need to revisit childhood haunts and memories, the other part of him wished she'd let them go and concentrate on the future, not a past she couldn't change.

"Good plan," she said, as Mason let out an ear-piercing pterodactyl screech of approval. She rubbed her ear. "On second thought, maybe you can hang out with the kids and I'll take care of the luggage. I don't want to lose hearing in my other ear."

John chuckled. "I don't either. Rock-paper-scissors? Best two out of three gets to choose." Mason let out another shriek, while the person behind them blasted their car horn. "Or we can all pile out now and get this done together."

Celeste kissed him. "Best plan yet."

Two hours later, John lay on the hotel bed giving Mason his bottle. Olivia was snuggled up against him, and Celeste was in the bathroom finishing her shower. Surrounded by the scent of baby soap and the warmth of his kids' tiny bodies, John could fall asleep. He wasn't ready for bed though, and wanted to talk with Celeste once the kids were sleeping. This would be their first family vacation. Again, he would rather have traveled to someplace tropical, but the point of a family vacation was to be with family. He needed to focus on that, not the location of the trip. Celeste needed to as well.

When he'd first met her, the attraction had been instantaneous and he'd easily fallen in love with her. Six months ago, when she'd been battling the evil ghost who'd eventually possessed him, he had briefly become one with her spirit, her soul melding with his. After that experience, and everything that had followed since, the word 'love' now seemed too generic. The magnitude of what they'd been through had stirred so many new emotions within him, yet he couldn't say with certainty what they were. All he knew was that after touching Celeste's soul, experiencing the beauty of her love, her goodness, he couldn't be without her, and that his emotions for her were bigger than him. Not overwhelming or complex, but necessary for his survival.

Which was why he wished she would let go of what had happened to him. Vigo "The Wolf" Donati, a small-time gangster who'd died in 1925, had taken possession of John's body for nearly three months. Celeste had held herself accountable because after she'd fought Vigo and won, she'd thought she had sent him to Hell. Instead, Vigo had been given an opportunity to take over John's body. John knew Celeste was wrestling with demons he couldn't tame. Knew they belonged to her, and that only she could make them disappear. Still, he wanted to make it clear he had no regrets, hadn't once blamed her for the possession, but actually embraced the entire ordeal. Because of Vigo and all that had followed, he now had a better understanding of Celeste's psychic world, which he would need since Olivia had her mother's gift. Mason might, too.

He glanced down at his son. Mason's eyes were closed and a small amount of formula dribbled from his mouth. John set the empty bottle aside, then used the pad of his thumb to wipe it away. He looked to Olivia, whose eyes were also closed, and kissed her forehead.

When Celeste exited the bathroom wearing only her bra and panties, he held a finger to his lips. "They're both sleeping."

"Thank God." She pulled a T-shirt and capri yoga pants from the overnight bag. "I was worried being in an unfamiliar place would keep them both up late."

"Now we know how to get them to go to bed quickly. All we have to do is go on a hellacious two-hour drive, swim for an hour, then give them a warm bath."

Celeste finished dressing, then sat on the edge of the bed. "Is that all?" She grinned. "That sounds wonderful."

John gently rolled Mason so he could rub the baby's back and hopefully get a little burp from him. "You know what would be wonderful? A beer."

"Let me wave my wand and produce a bottle for you."

"No, allow me." He twirled his index finger toward one of the tote bags filled with baby gear. "Presto. Go check the bag."

With a sexy smirk and a raised brow, she slid off the bed. Seconds later, she pulled out a bottle of wine, along with an opener. "While I'm amazed by your magical powers, you're not a very good magician. I thought you wanted a beer."

"I do, but I also know you would prefer wine. So, I used my powers to make my beautiful wife happy."

"You're such a sweet magician. Can you make the bottle cold and also produce wine glasses?"

"I would, but I don't want to waste my powers." When Mason burped loudly, John chuckled. "That's my boy."

"Again with bodily functions?" Celeste wrinkled her nose as she set the bottle and opener on the nightstand. "I'm glad he's sleeping. I don't want you encouraging him to be gross."

John continued to rub Mason's back. "He's a boy. He's supposed to be gross. Better he learns it from his father than some toddler at the park."

Grinning, she shook her head. "I don't know what to do with you."

"If we weren't sleeping with two kids, I know exactly what I'd do to you."

"Then maybe we should save the wine for tomorrow evening when we're at the rental," she suggested.

"I'll buy more. I wouldn't mind having a couple glasses with you and talking."

Understanding filled her eyes, "There are mugs by the coffee maker, and I could go down the hall and get some ice. Here," she said, reaching for Mason. "I'll put him in the crib."

"That's okay. Let him lie here for a few more minutes."

She smiled and brushed her fingers along Mason's dark hair. "He does look good on you." She leaned down and gave John a kiss, then toed on a pair of flip flops. "I'll be right back," she said after taking the ice bucket off the small desk.

When the door clicked shut, John continued to enjoy snuggling with his kids, but was done watching Liv's cartoons. Without disturbing Olivia, he raised the remote and began channel surfing. As the minutes passed, he wondered why Celeste hadn't returned to the room. The ice machine was located at the center of the hallway, near the elevators which were about ten doors from their room.

He flipped the channel, stumbled onto ESPN and caught the current score of the Cubs game. Olivia stretched. Oddly, Mason did, too. As he shifted slightly to move off the bed and put Mason in the portable crib, his son's eyes opened. His dark gaze holding concern, Mason stared at John.

"What's the matter, buddy?"

Mason's lower lip shot out, he released a little whimper and twisted his head toward Olivia. John glanced over at Liv, who was now seated and gaping at them, her eyes wide, glistening with tears and filled with fright.

"Liv, honey, what's wrong?"

"Mommy," she cried, then fell forward and let out a heart-wrenching sob.

Mason joined her. Opened his mouth wide and wailed harder than he had during the drive.

John quickly sat on the bed. Rocking Mason, he ran his hand along Olivia's back. "Mommy went down the hall to get ice," he assured her. "She'll be right back."

"No! I want Mommy," Olivia shouted, then hiccupped. "She gone!"

Mason's face grew red as he continued to cry. Needing Celeste back inside the room, John got off the bed, then placed Mason in the portable crib. While his kids bawled, he hurried to the door and, keeping it open with his leg, leaned into the hallway. Though tempted to yell for Celeste, he also didn't need people complaining about the noise, which they'd probably do anyway since the kids weren't quiet criers.

When he didn't see her, he went back inside the room, noticed Celeste had left her phone on the charger in the bathroom, and moved to the nightstand. He picked up the room phone and called the front desk.

"Good evening, this is Leslie, how can I help you?"

"Hi, is the third floor ice machine broken?" he asked, now wondering if Celeste had gone to a different floor.

"No one has called about it. As far as I know, it's working just fine. But I can send someone from maintenance to check on it for you."

"That's okay." He covered his ear in order to hear the woman over the kids. "My wife left the room a few minutes ago to get ice, and she's not back yet. I noticed you have a vending area by the front desk. Is she down there? She has blond curly hair, and is wearing black pants and a gray T-shirt."

"Sorry, but no one has walked through the foyer in the past twenty minutes. Are you sure she's not at the ice machine? It's in a little alcove, so you wouldn't be able to see her from the doorway."

The woman had a point, but it still shouldn't take Celeste this long to get ice. Unless...oh, God. If Celeste had fallen into a trance, she could be passed out on the floor or, even worse, roaming the building. Except she'd learned to control that aspect of her gift. Then again, she had also been extremely stressed and, in the past, anxiety had triggered some of her trances.

"Sir, do you want me to send someone to check on your wife? It sounds like you have your hands full."

He looked over his shoulder just as Liv finished putting on her tennis shoes and adjusted the Velcro straps. "That's okay. I'm going to take the kids and find her." After thanking the woman, he hung up the phone and turned to Olivia. "What are you doing?"

She stood and, after using her arm to wipe her red face and nose, she pulled in a ragged breath. "Find Mommy. She gone."

Hiding his concern, he opened the stroller. "Mommy's not *gone*." He took Mason from the crib and placed him in the stroller. "She's somewhere in the hotel. We'll find her together, okay?"

Olivia shook her head. "Her go bye-bye in car."

John snatched the van's keys from Celeste's purse. "No, honey. Mommy didn't drive off in the van."

"Car," she shouted, which made Mason start crying again.

"Enough, Olivia." He slammed the keys on the nightstand. "Now you listen to Daddy. Mommy is *here*. You need to stop and let me think."

Damn it, where the hell was Celeste? After putting on his tennis shoes and pocketing his phone and hotel keycard, he glanced around the room. He remembered to grab a blanket for Mason and Liv's stuffed alligator toy, Vlad. He handed her the toy. "Come on, let's go," he said, pulling the stroller backwards toward the door.

Olivia picked up the keys.

"We're not getting in the van."

Olivia's chin trembled and her eyes filled with tears. "Please? Mommy go bye-bye."

John took the keys from her and put them in his pocket. "Stop. Be a big girl and help take care of Mason while Daddy finds Mommy."

"No!" She grabbed John's hand. "Bye-bye."

"Liv, you need to stop..."

The walls and floor tilted. John's vision blurred. His surroundings spun and were sucked away as if a powerful vacuum were attached to the room. His head filled with a cacophony of distorted music and voices. The swirling quickened, made him nauseous, made his head hurt.

"Daddy?"

Olivia's voice filled his head.

"Right here, honey. Just give me a second. Daddy doesn't feel well."

The swirling came to an abrupt stop. The room went black, silent.

"What's happening?" John whispered, and tried to keep his fear in check. This was how it had begun when he'd been possessed. It couldn't be happening again. He didn't know where his wife was, or when she'd be back, and if something was invading his body, who would look after his kids?

"Olivia?" he called, hoping to God she could still hear him, that it was *him* speaking and not something or someone else.

A tiny light flickered up ahead. *"Daddy see?"* Olivia asked.

"See what?"

"Mommy."

A powerful force thrust John forward. The earlier sounds returned, along with the hum of an engine. Lights flashed around him, touching on a foggy haze. Then everything came into focus...

Celeste lay on a thin black carpet, her eyes closed, her wrists and ankles bound and her mouth sealed with silver tape. Muffled voices mingled with music from an oldies station, while lights occasionally touched along her face and body.

The image was abruptly sucked from his mind. Bright lights needled his eyes. He blinked several times and looked down, just as Olivia pulled her hand from his.

"Her gone," she said, sadness in her tone.

His mind racing, his gut twisting with dread, John stared at his daughter. "Did you...show me Mommy?" he asked, not sure if she'd really given him a glimpse of where Celeste was currently, or if she'd planted her own fears in his head. But how would Liv even come up with an image like that?

Olivia nodded. "I not bad girl."

The day after he'd been free of Vigo, he'd sworn Olivia had somehow gotten in his head and talked to him with her mind, not her mouth. Several times over the past few weeks, he'd tried to coax her into doing it again, but she never had, leading him to believe he'd imagined the whole thing. But now... He should be shocked that his three-year-old daughter could communicate with her mind and share a psychic vision. Except, after everything he'd been through with Celeste, nothing surprised him.

Crouching in front of his daughter, he rested a hand on her shoulder. "No, you're a good girl. Did you see who took her?"

"Miss Santa Claus shot Mommy."

"What?" John's mouth went dry. "What do you mean *shot*?"

Olivia stabbed the tip of her little index finger into John's bicep. "Mommy gots shot like baby Mason."

Meaning a needle, not a gun.

Thank God.

"Her haf white hair and red shirt," Olivia continued, and made circles with her fingers and held them over her eyes. "Big glasses."

Listening to a psychic three-year-old explain the alleged kidnapping of her mother was not going to work. "Was someone with Miss Santa Claus?"

She bobbed her head again. "Man haf hat," she answered, and touched her head.

"Just one man?"

"Mmm-hmm. He say grandma. Livy say Grammy Cami."

John stared at his daughter. His father-in-law, and owner of CORE, the investigation agency where John worked, was engaged to Camilla 'Cami' Carlyle, who Olivia called Grammy Cami. "The man was with his grandma?"

She shrugged.

John sat on the edge of the bed and shifted his gaze from his daughter to his son. Like Olivia, Mason stared at him, the look in his dark eyes strangely…mature. He didn't know what was going on with his kids or Celeste, but sitting around the hotel room wouldn't get him anywhere. Except, if the image Olivia showed him had or was actually happening, Celeste wasn't in the hotel. Based on what he'd seen, he suspected she was in a car and could now be miles away.

Before he jumped to any conclusions, he needed to check the hotel first. With the kids in tow, he left the room. When they reached the alcove where the ice machine was located and found it empty, they headed for the stairwell. John left the stroller on the landing, locking the wheels in place, then looked over the railing. No one was there. During the next ten minutes, he and the kids checked each floor until they reached the lobby. Once there, and trying desperately to hold onto his cool, he approached the front desk. The brunette's nametag indicated she was Leslie, the woman he'd spoken to earlier.

"Can I help you?" she asked.

"I called about my missing wife."

"Missing? You said she went to get ice. Are you sure she's not on any of the other floors?"

"I checked them and the stairwell."

"Is she outside smoking?" Leslie asked.

With his stomach sick with worry, and the image of Celeste bound and unconscious on his mind, he shook his head and remained calm for the kids. "She doesn't smoke, didn't take her purse, phone or the keys to the van. Could you have maintenance search the grounds and parking lot? I would, but I don't want to take the kids with me, and I need to call the police."

"Police? Sir, I'm sure your wife—"

"Mommy gone."

Leslie looked to Olivia, then to him. John had worked in law enforcement for nearly fifteen years. He'd interviewed hundreds of witnesses and suspects, and had learned to read body language. This woman not only didn't believe him, but her eyes said she suspected he was up to no good.

Screw her.

Angry and scared, the need to take action pulsed through him. "I'll handle this on my own," he said, taking Olivia's hand and pushing the stroller away from the desk.

They left the lobby and went outside into the warm night. He parked the stroller next to a bench, sat Olivia down on it and reached for his cell phone. He tapped on the screen, pulled up his father-in-law's number and hit call.

Within seconds, Ian answered. "You're supposed to be on vacation. This better not be about work."

"I don't know what's happening," John began, then explained everything, including what Olivia had showed him.

"Olivia *showed* you Celeste?" Ian's voice held disbelief. "Are you sure? You've been…different since the possession. So has Celeste. Maybe—"

"I'm going to stop you right there." Since his kids were watching him, John tamped down his anger. "Don't blow me any BS. I *know* you have a file on Olivia."

"I don't know what you're talking about."

"Don't deny it. Vigo told me. He saw it when he was looking through your office and said you also have files on Celeste, her mother and me. I get why you'd have files on us, but not Liv. How did you know she has the psychic gene? Celeste said she never told you."

The line went silent for a moment, then Ian replied, "Maxine."

John didn't believe him. Maxine was Celeste's close friend, her mentor, and he couldn't imagine the woman betraying Celeste's trust. "If you don't want to tell me the truth, then don't. Just make a call to the local FBI field office for me, and have them send people here. If you have any contacts with the Madison PD, that'd be helpful, too. We need to view footage from the security cameras. We need to confirm the man and old woman are responsible, and get a make on their vehicle."

"I know Madison's Chief of Police. I'll make the calls. Where are you staying?" After John gave him the name and address of the hotel, Ian released a breath. "I'll also call Hudson. We'll take the jet and be there within an hour. We need to get the kids back to Chicago. Cami can watch them while we search for Celeste."

"Olivia stays with me," John said, hoping his daughter would give him another glimpse of Celeste, this time with landmarks to help identify what direction the kidnappers were heading.

"John, you're certain about what Olivia showed you?"

He glanced to Olivia, who looked at him expectantly. "My

gut's telling me something is wrong. Celeste wouldn't walk out on us. You know that."

No, she'd fight to the death to be with her family.

✧ ✧ ✧

JOHN STOOD IN the hotel security office with Madison detective, Lieutenant Kevin Bernard, and FBI Agent, Laura Grabowski. Mason slept in the stroller and Olivia had fallen asleep on the cot Leslie had brought into the room. Once the police and FBI had shown up thirty minutes ago, and Leslie and her supervisor had discovered John worked for a criminal investigation agency, the hotel employees had gone from being suspicious to concerned and extremely cooperative, allowing them access to hotel records and security footage. Lieutenant Bernard had also brought several patrol officers with him and had them inspecting the parking lot and grounds, where they'd immediately found an empty hotel ice bucket in the hedges. Meanwhile, another detective was checking the businesses located near the hotel for additional security surveillance, with the hope they could get a hit on the kidnappers' car.

While the hotel security guard rewound the surveillance videos to the approximate time when Celeste had gone missing, John stepped out of the stuffy room and leaned against the wall. He pushed a hand through his hair and closed his eyes. The moment he did, he once again saw his wife bound and gagged. He pushed himself off the wall and scrubbed a hand down his face. As an FBI agent and investigator for CORE, he'd been involved in several kidnapping cases. Now he truly understood the pain and utter terror the victims' families had dealt with while their loved ones had been missing. The not knowing was killing him, driving a stake through his heart and shredding his insides.

Who had her? Why had they taken her? What did they plan to do to his wife?

He knew he needed to think like a cop, not a worried husband, but each time he looked at his children, the worry consumed him and fed his fears. Olivia and Mason needed their mother, just as much as he needed Celeste, and he didn't want to let down his children. But what if he couldn't find her? What if her kidnappers... He would *not* go there. They would find Celeste. Failure was not an option.

The lobby doors opened. Ian stepped inside, along with Hudson, fellow CORE agent Dante Russo, and Celeste's sister, Eden. The men wore grim expressions, but the fear in Ian's eyes disturbed him. Ian Scott never showed fear. He was the foundation of CORE, their arrogant, manipulative and fearless leader. But he was also a father, and Celeste was his only child.

Eden rushed over to John and hugged him. "Any word?" she asked.

"Nothing yet," he replied, then told them what the other investigators were doing to help find Celeste.

Ian stepped closer, until their group formed a tight circle. "You didn't tell them about Olivia, correct?"

John shook his head. "Absolutely not."

"What about Olivia?" Dante asked.

Dante and his wife, Jessica, were good friends. Years ago, their infant daughter had been kidnapped, but last fall, Celeste had helped them find her. Except, Dante and Jessica had no idea that Celeste's psychic gift was what had led her to the little girl. Celeste didn't deny she could communicate with the dead, but she also didn't advertise it, and very few CORE employees knew of her special ability.

"My wife is a psychic medium, so is our daughter."

Dante stared at him, his brow furrowed, his eyes holding concern. "I knew about Celeste, but hadn't realized Olivia has her gift."

"How did you know?" John asked.

"Everyone at CORE knows." Dante rested a hand on John's shoulder. "Did you really think you could keep something like that secret?"

No, he hadn't, and John wasn't surprised they knew. CORE

was a tight-knit group of investigators. And they weren't just co-workers, but close friends. "Olivia showed me Celeste, unconscious and bound in the back of a car. She also claims she saw the kidnappers."

"Anything we can use to find them?"

John considered Miss Santa Claus and the man in a hat, and shook his head. "No, but from how Liv explained it, I think they injected Celeste with a drug to incapacitate her."

Tears filled Eden's eyes as she took Hudson's hand. "My God," she whispered, leaning into her husband. "Where are the kids?"

"They're sleeping in the security guard's office."

"Give me your room key," Eden said, holding out her hand. "I'll get their things and take them home with me. Hud can drive us to the airfield."

John rubbed the back of his neck where tension stiffened his muscles. While he wanted his kids safe, comfortable and somewhere familiar, he was afraid to let them go. Especially Olivia. What if she had another vision? What if she was able to show him the kidnappers' faces or location? Even worse, what if his daughter saw them hurting her mother?

"I'd like to keep Liv with me. Right now, she's my only connection to Celeste."

"But she's three," Eden argued. "John, she doesn't understand what she can do, or what's happening to her mom."

"She knows damned well what's happened," John said with vehemence. "She's the one who convinced me Celeste was taken. I get why you want to take her home, but understand this...I *need* Olivia with me. I've solved multiple investigations with Celeste's help. Now I plan to find my wife with Olivia's."

"And I know what Celeste can see. Do you really want Liv to see those things? To witness what's happening to her mom?" A tear slipped down Eden's cheek. "She's just a baby."

John touched Eden's arm. "I have to get my wife back."

"I don't want to subject my granddaughter to any of this," Ian said, "but I agree with John."

It didn't matter to John who agreed with him, Olivia was his child. No one would tell him what he could or could not do where she was concerned. He pulled the keycard from his pocket, then handed it to Eden. "Mason's things are in the small blue bag. His diaper bag is up there, too."

Eden's hand trembled as she took the card. After Hudson volunteered to go with her, the two left the lobby for the elevator.

The moment they disappeared around the corner, Agent Grabowski stepped from the security office. "John, you're going to want to see this."

His stomach tightened with nervous energy as he headed into the room, Dante and Ian behind him. Olivia still slept on the cot, and Mason hadn't woken, either. John looked from his children to the four small monitors on the wall above the desk. "What do you have?" John asked after introducing Ian and Dante.

Detective Bernard pointed to the still shot on the far left monitor. "This is from the first floor's west entrance, just outside the stairwell."

John glanced to the timestamp which read six thirty-three p.m. "Celeste went missing shortly after eight."

"I know. Just watch," Bernard said, as the security guard hit PLAY.

Within seconds, a woman with white hair, large glasses and wearing an over-sized red windbreaker appeared outside the glass door. A black man with a clean-shaven head also approached the door from the outside. He spoke with the woman for a moment, then used a keycard to open the door. After letting the woman inside, he headed down the hallway and out of range of the camera. The woman, whose features were undeterminable, remained at the door until yet another man—wearing a baseball hat pulled down low and hiding his face—arrived, at which point she glanced around the hallway before letting him inside the building.

"I've seen that woman before," John said as the video was paused.

"Leslie, the clerk from the front desk, recognized her, too," Bernard said. "She couldn't ID the man in the hat, but remembers the guy who let the older woman into the hotel. I have an officer heading to his room now to bring him down here for questioning."

"Where did you see the woman?" Agent Grabowski asked. "Leslie doesn't believe she's staying here."

"When we arrived. I was in the van with the kids, waiting for Celeste outside the lobby. Celeste held the door open for the old woman."

"So you saw her face and can describe her."

"No." John kept his focus on the screen. "She was hunched over and her head was down. I didn't see her face. But I remember white hair and the chains hanging from her glasses."

Bernard leaned toward the monitor. "I didn't notice the chains until now." He glanced to the security guard. "Is there a way to zoom in on an image?"

The man shook his head. "Not with our equipment."

"Our forensics people might be able to do something with the video," Agent Grabowski said. "Let's move on to the next one."

This video had been cued to seven twenty-five p.m. The older woman—who was no longer hunched over or shuffling—and the man in the hat exited the stairwell at the far end of the hotel hallway. They both kept their heads lowered when they walked, then quickly turned their backs on the camera and acted as if they were getting ready to enter one of the rooms. The elevator doors opened. Carrying Mason, Celeste stepped into the hallway, followed by Olivia and John, who held a pizza box.

"We'd just finished swimming in the hotel pool," John said, watching as he and his family walked out of range of the camera. "I had a pizza delivered to the lobby." The woman and man turned away from the door and stared after John and his family. The couple then walked past the elevators and into the alcove where the ice machine was located.

The guard fast-forwarded the video until Celeste's image appeared. Wearing black capri yoga pants, a gray T-shirt and flip flops, she carried the small ice bucket. John's chest tightened as he kept his gaze locked on the screen, waiting, anticipating the moment when the couple would overpower his wife. When Celeste disappeared into the alcove, other than Mason's soft snores, the room became eerily quiet. Moments later, the old woman stepped back into the hallway.

"Pause it," John said, moving closer to the monitor. "What's she putting in her purse?"

Detective Bernard had the guard rewind the video, then press PLAY. "Looks like a pen."

Miss Santa Claus shot Mommy.

Anger settled in John's chest, making him burn with hatred. "Or a syringe," he said, as the man, holding Celeste's arm around his shoulders, dragged her into the hallway.

Celeste tried to walk, staggered as if drunk, and lost one of her flip flops. The old lady picked up the shoe, then proceeded down the hallway with the man and Celeste. When they reached the stairwell, the man bent at the knees, then lifted Celeste over one of his shoulders. Her body dangled along the man's back, her hair and arms swaying.

Bernard had the guard stop the video. "Watch the third monitor," he said, telling the guard to press PLAY. "You can see them carrying her out of the building and into the parking lot."

The setting sun brightened the screen, making the images grainy and blurry. "Do you have another view of the parking lot?" John asked the security guard as the old woman opened the back driver's side door and the man quickly placed Celeste's limp body inside a late-model, black SUV.

"Not of this particular area," the guard replied. "And the other parking lot cameras are aimed toward the building, so you won't be able to see the vehicle driving away."

When the SUV vanished from the screen, Bernard had the guard stop the tape. "Let's hope one of my guys finds a business that also has video surveillance. Looks like they're driving a Jeep, but I want a plate number."

Leslie knocked on the door as she entered the room. "I found the hotel guest who let in the woman. His name is Anthony Marks."

"Send him in," Detective Bernard said.

With a nod, Leslie left and, within seconds, presented them with the man they'd seen on the surveillance footage. "This is Anthony Marks," she said.

Bernard pointed to a still shot of the old woman. "Mr. Marks, do you recognize this woman?"

The man nodded. "Yeah. She was searching her purse, trying to find her key so she could get into the building." He darted his gaze around the room, settling it on Bernard's badge. "I wouldn't have let her in, but she was old and harmless, so I didn't think much of it."

The woman definitely wasn't harmless. As for being old, John wasn't sure about that, either. She could have been wearing a wig and makeup to disguise her real age. "Did you get a good look at her face?"

Marks explained that he'd been in a hurry and hadn't paid attention to what she'd looked like. He hadn't seen the man with her, or their car. Bernard dismissed him, but contacted one of his detectives to tell him about the Jeep. Twenty minutes later, an officer came into the room.

"Sir," he said to Bernard, "the convenience store cameras caught the Jeep leaving the hotel parking lot. We were able to read the Ohio license plate."

"Let's run it," Bernard said, standing.

"Already done. But, it was reported stolen last night from a Motel 6 in Toledo."

John leaned against the wall. Celeste had been gone for nearly ninety minutes. If the kidnappers weren't local, and based on the stolen Ohio license plate that was a solid assumption, they could now be sixty plus miles from Madison.

In which direction had they gone? Where were they taking

Celeste and for what purpose?

"We need to contact Toledo PD and find out if anyone was reported missing last night," John said, staying in cop-mode, and keeping his fears from making him insane with worry. "Taking women from hotels might be their MO."

Bernard glanced to the officer. "Get on it," he said, then faced John. "You're sure you never saw the Jeep during your drive from Chicago? Is there any reason why someone might target your wife?"

Between his career with the FBI and CORE, John had helped incarcerate dozens of criminals. Had someone decided to get even with him by going after his wife? Maybe. But where to begin?

He quickly thought back to the time when Ian and Cami had been kidnapped, then hunted. John and the other CORE agents had spent hours poring over files with the hope of discovering who had targeted Ian or Cami. They didn't have hours. With each minute that passed, Celeste could be driven farther away from them.

"It's possible she was taken in retaliation for something I've done, or because of someone I helped arrest." John rubbed the tension at the base of his neck. "We can have our agents look into potential suspects, but I think our focus for now should be on the Jeep and couple."

"Agreed." Bernard started for the door. "We'll put out a BOLO for the Jeep and the couple."

"We can use Celeste's driver's license photo and post that, too," Agent Grabowski suggested, and turned to the detective. "Can we get your forensics team here? I think we should have them search for any trace evidence by the ice machine and see if they can get any prints off the doors we saw the couple touch."

Mommy sleeping.

When Olivia's voice filled his head, John turned toward the cot. His daughter was still lying there, but her eyes were open and on him. He waited until the officer, detective and agent left the room, then knelt next to Olivia. Before Celeste had begun working with Maxine, her psychic visions would come to her in her dreams. Now he wondered if Olivia was experiencing the same thing. "Did you see Mommy sleeping while *you* were sleeping?" he asked, smoothing a blond curl from her face.

She nodded and pulled her thumb from her mouth. "It dark."

"Well, it's nighttime." He gave her what he hoped was a reassuring smile. "Did you see Miss Santa Claus or the man?"

"Uh-uh." She touched her ear. "Livy hear. She...she say, 'go fast' an man say, 'stop wagging'. That funny." She scrunched her nose. "Doggy wag tail, not Grammy Cami."

John let out a breath. Using Olivia to help him could prove difficult. Three-year-olds had their own language, one he was still trying to get used to understanding. "No, Grammy Cami doesn't have a tail to wag, so maybe the man was telling Miss Santa Claus to not nag him."

She shrugged, then looked toward the door when Eden and Hudson entered the room. Liv's gaze immediately dropped to Eden's rounded stomach, where her pregnancy was just starting to show, then she shifted her focus to Ian and smiled. "Hi, Grandpa."

The worry lining Ian's face intensified and his eyes filled with sadness. He approached Olivia. "Hi, honey," he said, linking his pinky with hers as they always did when they saw each other.

Olivia stared intently at her grandfather, then the corner of her mouth tilted in a knowing smile. "Grandpa gots a secret."

CHAPTER 3

The Ryker Residence, Silver Spring, Maryland
Saturday, 12:02 p.m. Eastern Daylight Time

"*WAKE UP. HURRY! Before they come.*"

Celeste fluttered her heavy eyelids, then squeezed them shut against the harsh light. Her head ached. Her mind was muddled with quick flashes of memories…driving in the minivan, Mason crying and vomiting, swimming at the hotel, a large ice machine. Groggy, dizzy, wondering if she'd drunk too much wine last night, she licked her dry lips.

And panicked.

She couldn't lick, couldn't move her mouth. She opened her eyes. The blinding light caused her vision to blur into tiny dots, making everything in the room fuzzy silhouettes. Blinking several times, she reached for her lips and froze. Quickly looked down the length of her body. Instead of seeing her torso and legs, as if she'd been caught off guard by the flash of a camera, the afterimage of the indistinct objects remained, though brighter, more colorful. She shook her head and blinked again until the room came into focus.

Her heart pounded hard. Her breath quickened. Terror tore through her, cramped her stomach with nausea and had acid burning her throat. She was dressed in a hospital gown. Restraints held down her legs, waist and chest. A chill washed over her. She raised her head and glanced around the room. Took in the nightstand and dresser propped against a cinder block wall that had been painted white. Two small, glass block windows let in little sunlight, but the large, rectangular fluorescent fixture above her made the room almost unbearably bright. She looked toward her bare feet. Along the far wall stood a tall metal utility cabinet. To her left was a closed door and…

A teenage girl shoved her pale face near Celeste's. Startled, Celeste stiffened and tried to ease away. The restraints wouldn't allow her.

The girl's long white hair framed her hollow cheeks, while her milky-blue translucent eyes studied Celeste with concern. Glancing toward the door, the teenager moved back. When shades of grays and yellows surrounded her lithe body clad in a hospital patient's gown, deep sadness settled on Celeste's chest. She'd interacted with many ghosts, but the young ones always bothered her the most. Especially if they'd died violently.

"They'll be here soon. We don't have much time." The girl's voice filled Celeste's head. *"Why are you back?"*

Back? Frustrated she couldn't speak, confused and uncertain where she was and why she was restrained, she grunted against whatever sealed her mouth.

The girl, whom she placed at around seventeen or eighteen, hovered closer, her white brows pulling together, her gaze bewildered. *"Speak with your mind."*

What was she talking about? Celeste wasn't telepathic. She wasn't even sure if telepathy was possible.

She shook her head and grunted again.

"Of course it's possible. We've communicated this way before."

Celeste froze. Had the girl just read her mind?

"I did. I'm Karen. Don't you remember me?" she asked, her tone heavy with disappointment. *"It's been many years, I think. I…I'm not sure. My memory isn't very good anymore. But I could never forget you, Janice. You were so sweet and caring, and tried so hard to help us."*

Janice? How could this girl have known her mother?

The door opened. A middle-aged man with short brown hair, blue eyes and an easy smile entered, along with an elderly woman, whose hair was as white as the ghost beside Celeste.

"Mother? No, Janice. You've just forgotten." The girl vanished only to reappear at the foot of the bed. *"It's there. Open your mind and remember. Last time you saw Aiden, he was a little boy. And his grandma, Martha, had salt and pepper hair. Do you remember what Martha's son tried to do to you? What he was doing to all of us? Janice, you need to open your mind."*

Celeste hadn't a clue who these people were, how her mother had been involved with them, or what had happened to Karen. What she did know was fear. And right now, with the way Aiden smiled at her, stared at her as if she were a coveted prize, pure terror kept her paralyzed. Opened her mind and unleashed memories...

Holding the door for the old woman as she'd exited the hotel. Seeing her later by the ice machine, along with the man. A hand being clamped over her mouth. Struggling as the old woman had pierced her flesh with a needle.

Aiden tore the tape from Celeste's mouth, stinging her lips and skin. As she dragged in a deep breath, more memories quickly surfaced...

The darkness, brief flashes of headlights, music from an oldies station, being forced to pee in a bedpan while in the back of a car. Another piercing from a needle.

They'd drugged her, but how many times? What was the drug and did it have lasting side effects? How long ago had they kidnapped her?

And *why* her? Why did they take her? Did John know?

Oh, God. John...the kids. He must be worried sick. Damn it, hadn't they been through enough? They were supposed to be on vacation, enjoying each other and family time with Olivia and Mason.

"I'm sure you have plenty of questions for us," Aiden began. "Now that you're awake and comfortable in your bed, let me start by introducing myself."

"Aiden," Celeste whispered, her throat dry and raw. She

looked to the old woman. "Martha."

Aiden rubbed his arms and smiled. "Oh, she's good," he said, glancing to Martha.

Looking bored, Martha slipped on her glasses, which had been dangling around her neck, and studied Celeste. "She could have heard us talking."

"I never call you Martha," Aiden said.

"True, but remember how I told you about the minister's wife? When I was repeating what she'd said to me, I think I might've said my name."

Aiden frowned. "She was drugged almost the entire time we were driving."

Martha shrugged. "Drugs affect each of us differently. Before we decide which procedure to start with, I think we should see what she can do. That's how your father always began."

The ghost remained at the foot of the bed. The yellow of her aura was becoming bolder, the gray darker. Karen darted her gaze from Aiden and Martha to Celeste. *"I don't understand,"* she said. *"Martha knows what you can do. She was here with her son."*

Celeste ignored the ghost. Later, when they were alone, she'd question the girl. Right now, she needed to pay close attention to Aiden and Martha. Procedure, experiments…those two words wouldn't settle well with her even if she were seeing her regular doctor. Since she doubted the old lady or her grandson were medics, she needed to steel herself for whatever they planned to do with her.

"Good idea," Aiden said. "We know Janice was a clairvoyant medium who was also telepathic."

Martha took off her glasses and let them hang from the beaded chain. She leaned down and studied Celeste as if she were a specimen. "Can you get inside my head?" she asked, her eyes glittering with excitement.

"I'm not telepathic. My mother wasn't, either." Celeste licked her lips and tasted the adhesive from the tape. "How did you know her?" she asked, unease working through her. Between what she'd read in her mom's journals, Karen calling her Janice and acting as if they knew each other, and Aiden and Martha's knowledge about her mom, Celeste knew the answer. These people had worked for Dr. Seth Ryker, the psychiatrist who had killed five people and attempted to experiment on her mom. Except that couldn't be right. The doctor had been sentenced to life in prison, without the possibility of parole.

"She was a patient." Martha smiled. "How is your mother?"

"Dead."

"What a shame." The old woman frowned, yet the anticipation brightening her eyes remained. "It would've been interesting to have Janice here, too. We could have performed simultaneous experiments."

Aiden walked to the metal cabinet. "Two test subjects with the exact same abilities would've been great. At least we have George, though."

"Yes, he'll have to do," Martha said. "Taking another person is too risky."

Aiden pulled a small piece of luggage, which reminded Celeste of a vintage train suitcase, out of the cabinet and carried it to a metal cart positioned near the bed. "But if Celeste is like her mother, I wonder if her little girl also has the gift?"

"I wonder." Martha's wrinkly face split into a grin, revealing bright white dentures. "Well, Celeste? Is your daughter also a psychic medium?"

Celeste hid her fear, kept her face stony. "No." She narrowed her eyes and let the hatred consume her. "She's a normal little girl. Don't you dare think about going near her. You don't know my husband or father. I'm warning you, if they find you…you will *not* go to prison."

"Will I go to my grave?" Martha's smile never faltered. "I turn eighty-six in October. Death doesn't scare me. Knowing my son could possibly die in prison does. And you, my dear, are going to help us get him out of there."

"That's right." Aiden rolled the cart until it touched the bed, then opened the case and pulled out the electrical cord attached to it. "If you give us your full cooperation, and once we've run all of our tests and proven my dad's theories, you'll be free to go," he said with a smile.

"He's lying!" Karen glared at Aiden. *"He's just like his father. If you don't find a way to escape, you will never leave."* The ghost met Celeste's gaze. *"You'll be like me."*

Celeste's mantra had always been, *the living are more powerful than the dead*. Right now, these two live people scared her more than any evil spirit she'd encountered. While she'd learned ghosts could harm her, these people could kill her.

"Did your mom ever tell you about my dad, Dr. Seth Ryker?" Aiden asked.

"I know all about your father," Celeste said, attempting to project confidence and be strong. "He kidnapped and killed people."

Aiden held up a finger. "Correction, he only kidnapped your mother, the rest were here as volunteers. And, technically, Janice came here on her own. My dad just didn't let her leave. As for killing people, those deaths were accidental and in the name of science."

Aiden was right. Seth Ryker and her mom had been colleagues, who'd both worked with the FBI. Dr. Ryker would create psychological profiles on criminals, while her mother had acted as a psychic consultant. Thirty-five years ago, Dr. Ryker had invited Janice to his house to discuss a case. Only the doctor hadn't been interested in the investigation, but in her mother's clairvoyant abilities. He'd claimed he could enhance her gift, make it go away or take a *normal* person and make them psychic.

She glanced to Karen. Now that she knew where she was, who had abducted her and why, she remembered the case file Ian had on the Ryker investigation. She recalled reading about Karen Webber, along with Dr. Ryker's two other victims. Very little had been written about Martha, and there'd been no mention of the son. As for Dr. Ryker's theories, she wasn't sure what to believe.

Was it possible he could take away a psychic gift and give it to someone else? Could he have taken her mother's abilities and strengthened them, made her telepathic? Fortunately, her mother had been rescued before Dr. Ryker's theories could be put to the test. Especially since Janice had been pregnant with Celeste at the time of the kidnapping.

Aiden finished plugging in the box, then turned it around, revealing a series of knobs labeled *Nerve, Muscle* and...*Voltage*. Her heart pounding harder, she glanced at Karen, who stared at the box, her transparent eyes filled with terror.

"Let me tell you a little something about my dad." Aiden sat on the edge of the bed. "The media labeled him a monster. His victims' families wanted his blood, and the state's attorney hoped for the death penalty. But Grandma and I have always known the truth. My father wasn't a monster. He was a genius, a man ahead of his time, a brilliant psychiatrist and parapsychologist who probably understood the human mind better than God." He narrowed his eyes. "And if it hadn't been for the FBI, specifically, *your* father, Ian Scott, my dad could've continued with his experimentation, worked for the government creating an army of super-spies, written books and articles. Hell, he could have won the Nobel Prize in Physiology or Medicine."

"That's right," Martha said with a nod.

"So we figured, why not make it true?" Aiden continued. "Why not finish the experiments my father started, and show the world that Dr. Seth Ryker is a valuable scientist who needs to be working rather than imprisoned?"

Oh, God. These people were insane. "Aiden, please listen to me," Celeste said, hoping she could talk sense into him and his grandmother. "Even if your father had continued with his work and was successful, no government agency would have backed a man who ran unethical, inhumane, and illegal experiments from his basement. Which is where I'm assuming you've brought me. And the idea of creating an army of *super-spies* is ridiculous."

"Really? Are you aware of the Stargate Project?"

"Yes, it was a failure." Back in the '70s, the CIA had created the program, but in the '90s, after spending millions of dollars researching *remote viewing* and placing psychic spies in the field, they'd terminated and declassified the unsuccessful project.

Aiden grinned. "It wouldn't have been if my dad had been part of their team."

He pulled headphones that had thick white cloth wrapped around the earpieces from the back of the box. They reminded Celeste of the electrodes used on Jack Nicholson in *One Flew Over the Cuckoo's Nest* when he'd been given electroshock therapy.

Electroshock therapy.

Panicking, terrified of what would happen to her once Aiden sent a jolt of electricity into her brain, she struggled against the restraints. "What is that thing?"

Aiden tapped the top of the box. "This is an electroshock therapy machine from 1945. But today's scientists don't use the term electroshock. I guess they think electroconvulsive therapy sounds a little less...*shocking*," he said with a grin.

"How is it you own one?" she asked, stalling for time while hoping to God a miracle would happen and sweep her far from this place. "After what your father did, I'd think the FBI took all of his equipment."

"Oh, they did. Can you believe I bought this on eBay for three hundred dollars?" Aiden placed the electrodes on her head so the cloth pieces rested along her temples. "I had to rebuild parts of it, but I can assure you it works just fine."

"He's right," Martha said, holding a mouth guard. "We've used it on our other subject without issue."

Celeste turned her head away from Martha and looked to Aiden. "Wait! Why would you give me electroconvulsive therapy without knowing what I can do? What if it does something to my psychic abilities? And if you're trying to enhance my gift, how will you know if you have or not?"

Aiden pressed his lips together and nodded. He looked to Martha and smiled. "You were right. Bringing out the machine makes people more pliable." He refocused on Celeste. "Okay, let's see what you can do."

"I told you, I'm not telepathic. I can see into the past and talk to ghosts."

"What about the future?"

"I've had a few rare moments, but they were very quick, vague images."

"And the present? Can you see hidden objects or people located a great distance away?"

"If you're referring to remote viewing, I've only been able to do that once. And I don't know how I did it."

"Telekinesis?"

Celeste shook her head.

Aiden sighed and crossed his arms over his chest. "Well, Grandma, what do you think? If she can't move objects with her mind or talk inside our heads, should we have her tell us something about our past?"

Martha shrugged. "Since I don't believe in ghosts, and I know for a fact the only thing haunting our house is your father's reputation, you might as well have her give you a reading."

Celeste shifted her gaze to the ghost hovering at the foot of the bed. If only Martha knew the truth.

Aiden dropped his arms to his sides. "This is disappointing. Dad said Janice was telepathic."

"Makes me wonder about V. Why would he claim the girl is stronger than the mother?" Martha narrowed her eyes and looked down on Celeste. "Unless she's holding out on us."

"I swear, I'm not." Celeste's stomach grew sick. "Who's V?"

"Don't know. A few weeks ago, we received a note about you and your mother, and it was simply signed, *V.*" Aiden cocked his head. "I'm assuming this person isn't a friend of yours."

A few weeks ago, John was still possessed by Vigo Donati. *Son of a bitch.* The bastard was gone, and yet he was still infecting their lives.

"Not in the least," she said.

"Do you know where we can find V?" Aiden asked. "I'd like to get in touch with him. Or is V a woman?"

She stared at Aiden. "Why, to thank him for telling you about me?"

"To tie up loose ends and make sure he's not setting us up," Martha said, drawing Celeste's attention.

Her fear escalated. These two were so desperate to find a way to release Dr. Ryker, they'd taken a major risk by trusting Vigo. Which made them not only insane, but reckless and foolish, too...an extremely dangerous combination. "I would've worried about that before I participated in a kidnapping."

"We don't owe you an explanation. Tell us where we can find V, or your therapy begins now."

"Hell. Vigo was a ghost."

"A ghost?" Martha hardened her jaw. "Aiden, turn on the machine."

"Wait," Celeste shouted. "I'm not lying. Vigo possessed my husband's body. During that time, he must've sent you the note."

"Possessed?" Martha looked to her grandson. "Zap her."

Celeste fisted her hands. "It's true. I swear. I know it sounds crazy, but it happened. I wasn't lying about being able to communicate with the dead. And Vigo was an evil spirit who refused to accept death."

Martha eyed her with skepticism. "Even if I believed you, which I don't, how would this Vigo know about my son, Seth?"

"I'm not sure," Celeste said, but assumed Vigo must've nosed around in Ian's files. But why would he contact the family of the man who'd kidnapped her mother and performed unethical human experiments? Then, when Celeste remembered how Vigo'd had an interest in her life insurance policy, she had her answer. Greed. With that bastard, it had always boiled down to greed.

"My dad was convinced Janice could also talk to ghosts." Aiden rested his rear on the bed again. "Maybe she's telling the truth."

Martha rolled her eyes. "Possession is ridiculous," she said with impatience. "Just have the girl give you a reading. We still need to check on George, and I have to finish the afghan I'm donating to the church's charity drive."

With a nod, Aiden touched Celeste's arm. "Okay, go ahead."

"I need an item you carry with you often." Celeste looked to his wristwatch. "Your watch will work, but I can't guarantee I'll be able to perform a reading. Not under this kind of pressure."

"If not," Aiden began, handing her the watch, "then a little shock therapy might get the psychic juices flowing."

Terrified he'd fry her brain, she closed her eyes, held the watch and tried to concentrate on what it could reveal about him. But before that familiar tug to her psyche came, her mind strayed…to John and the kids, to her mom, and even Vigo. She opened her eyes again and met Karen's ghostly gaze.

"Why aren't you saying anything?" Karen asked. *"Hurry, tell him something so he doesn't turn on the machine."*

"I can't," Celeste said, a tear slipping down her cheek. "I'm too scared and stressed to do this."

Martha released an exaggerated sigh. "Flip the switch. Maybe one hundred and fifty volts of electricity will motivate her to cooperate."

"Let's hope." Aiden reached for the watch, but Celeste gripped it tightly. He let her keep it, and leaned close to her face. "We have a lot riding on you. If it turns out you're nothing like Janice, and our experiments fall flat, then we won't have any leverage to get my dad out of prison." He pushed her bangs from her forehead. "Do you understand?"

Her heart racing, her head growing dizzy with the onslaught of a panic attack, Celeste nodded. She understood she would die in this place if she didn't find a way to escape or convince them to let her go. In the meantime, she needed to give them something. Anything to prove that she was of value to them and their experiments.

"Please," she begged. "I can give you a reading, just not like this. Take off the restraints. I won't run. I swear. I need to be seated in a comfortable position to give you what you want."

Aiden looked to Martha. "Should we let her?"

Martha glared at her. "No. She remains strapped to the bed."

"You heard Grandma." Aiden stood. "Do the reading as you are."

"You can do this," Karen encouraged her. *"You must! Relax."* Her eyes wide, frantic, the ghost glanced at the electrodes, before facing her. *"Please. You don't want them to turn on the machine."*

No, she didn't. She wanted to be with her family.

Celeste closed her eyes again and gripped the watch, set her fear aside, and concentrated on John. Her husband, his love and strength, had always kept her grounded, had helped her remain rooted in this world, and gave her a reason to not remain in the spirit realm. Drawing in a slow breath, she opened her mind. Focused on the watch, on Aiden, she sought that distorted plane between the present and the past.

A tug came to her psyche. Pulled at her mind, until she was swept into a colorful vortex. The walls around her spun with blurred images, converging at the center of the swirling eddy, where a bright light waited for her. She honed in on the light, drove toward it until she was propelled into it. The spinning walls fell away revealing a bright room. Muffled voices became clear as images sharpened…

Celeste glanced around the room. Armed, uniformed guards stood at every door, people sat at tables, some wearing orange jumpsuits and handcuffs, others in regular street clothes. She looked to the table next to her, and stared at the murderer and kidnapper, Seth Ryker.

"Ian Scott has a daughter?" Seth folded his hands, shifted his gaze from his son, Aiden, and mother, Martha, to one of the guards standing along the wall of what Celeste assumed was a prison visiting room. A small smile curved his mouth. "And you say she's stronger than her mother?" He shook his head and chuckled. "I'd like to see Scott suffer, but I'm not interested in revenge, and I'm not taking the bait. You don't know if this V person who wrote me works for Ian or the FBI. This could be a setup. Someone could be watching."

V. After everything Vigo had put her family through, after setting into motion what was happening to her now, she hated the dead man more than ever. She also wondered if he'd left behind any other nasty surprises before he'd been judged and sent to Hell.

Aiden stared at his dad for a moment, disappointment clear in his eyes. "I don't believe that. If this was a setup, why send the letter to the home address and not the prison. Whoever mailed this obviously doesn't realize you're still incarcerated. Plus, I went to Chicago and found the woman's home."

Dread slipped up Celeste's spine. Aiden had been watching her, stalking her. Could find her children if he wanted.

"She's married, has a couple of kids, owns a bakery," Aiden continued. "She's so...normal, I started to question the letter from V. Then I followed her to Maxine Morehouse's."

"Maxine?" Seth's eyes brightened with interest. "Such a fascinating creature," he said, then cleared his throat. "No. I told you, I'm not out for revenge, or interested in delving back into parapsychology. I forbid you to do anything but burn the letter."

Confused, Celeste stared at Seth. How did he know Maxine? And if Maxine knew about Dr. Seth Ryker, why hadn't she said anything to her? Celeste had told Maxine how her mother had met Ryker when she'd been working for the FBI, and how the man had kidnapped Janice with the intention of using her as a psychic human guinea pig. Unease settled over her, but she quickly shoved it aside. Ian and Maxine had met socially. Celeste's wealthy, eccentric mentor had never worked for the FBI and wouldn't know Dr. Ryker.

Martha's beaded eyeglass chain jiggled as she shook her snow-white head. "That won't do." She adjusted her oversized glasses, which looked to be from the '80s, and gave her son a stern look.

"Won't do?" Seth echoed. "No, what I won't tolerate is seeing my son sentenced to life in prison. I'm sixty-nine. I'll die in a cell. I don't want that for Aiden. Besides, my work is too complex for a layman to repeat."

"Too complex? Your son is a genius. And a doctor."

A genius doctor? Aiden hadn't given Celeste that impression. What genius would think psychic super-spies could be a real thing, or break multiple laws after receiving a vague note from a total stranger?

"Who can't practice medicine because he couldn't pass the boards," Seth countered.

Martha narrowed her eyes. "Aiden knows all about your experiments. He's studied your notes and can do this."

Seth nervously shifted his gaze to Aiden, then back to Martha. "He should only know what he's read in the papers or heard on the news."

"Oh, for Christ's sake." Martha let out an impatient sigh. "He's a grown man. And I'm proud of your work."

"But the FBI confiscated my files and journals," Seth argued.

"And months prior to the raid, I made copies of everything. It's all there. We can begin right where you left off and prove your theories as fact." Martha leaned closer to her son. "Seth, this isn't about revenge, but about salvaging your reputation. Salvaging your life."

"Grandma's right," Aiden said, finally joining the conversation. "If we prove to the world that you're not a psychopathic killer, but a brilliant scientist, maybe you'll have an opportunity for parole."

Martha patted Aiden's hand. "The boy has a valid point. Plus, you've already served thirty-five years and have been a model prisoner. You've paid your so-called debt to society."

Seth chuckled. "You two honestly believe that kidnapping Ian Scott's psychic daughter and running my experiments on her will give me an opportunity to leave this prison?" He looked to Aiden. "Do not listen to my mother about this."

"Why not?" Martha asked. "I know everything you've done. Remember, I served as your assistant, and was a nurse for nearly forty years. I might be eighty-five, but I can still help prep our patient."

"And I know what *you've* done," Seth said, his face growing red. "Leave my son out of this."

"What's the matter, dear? Do you no longer believe in your own theories? Have years of dealing with prison counselors convinced you that you're a quack? A serial killer with a degree in psychiatry?" Martha took off her glasses and let them dangle. She glanced around the prison visiting room. "Do you want this to be your legacy?" She placed a hand on Aiden's forearm. "Or do you want your legacy to shine through your son?"

"I don't want him going to prison," Seth repeated, his tone quiet, angry.

"Has anyone asked me what I want?" Aiden pulled his arm away from his grandmother, and held his father's concerned gaze. "I know I'm a disappointment to you, and have been since the moment I was diagnosed with Asperger's."

"That's not true."

"Dad, it's okay. I'm sure you had high hopes for me, but even with a high IQ I've managed to fail at everything. Medical school, two marriages, I can't keep a job and I live with my grandmother."

"You're not a disappointment," Seth assured him. "You've been a good son. I don't think there's an inmate here who gets as many letters, phone calls and visits as I do. No, I blame myself for the challenges you've faced in life. Had I not been selfish and focused on my patients and my work with the FBI, I would've never gone to prison. I would've been there to raise you."

"But you weren't," Aiden said, bitterness in his tone and sounding as if he were a whiney child. "I've never once been angry with you, or questioned what you've done. Not even when Grandma and I were dealing with the narrow-minded people of Silver Spring, the media, the bullying and threats. Because I believed in you, in everything Grandma told me about you. And if you hadn't tried to prove your theories, wouldn't you have always wondered? Don't you still wonder if you were on the right track?"

Guilt lined Seth's face as he shook his head. "I don't think about those days."

"I might've been ten when you were arrested, but I think about them all the time. How could you not?" Aiden asked. "You were a consultant to the FBI before profiling had a name. You helped agents capture killers."

"Then I became one."

"Not on purpose. Those deaths were accidental," Aiden said, holding up a hand when Seth opened his mouth to speak. "Grandma and I are going through with this. We will prove your theories are true, and I guarantee when the government hears about it, they'll be willing to make a trade. Our knowledge for your freedom."

"Please, son. I don't want you to suffer the same fate as me."

"I won't. Not with Grandma's help."

Seth glanced at Martha. *"Can I have a moment alone with Aiden?"*

"Grandma said you'd object to all of this. Maybe you're worried we'll succeed and the credit will go to us, not you." Aiden fisted his hands. *"We're in this together, so anything you have to say can be said in front of Grandma."*

As Seth let out a breath, he shook his head. *"I have nothing more to say on the subject."*

"Fine," Aiden said, with dissatisfaction. *"Maybe once the experimentation begins you'll change your mind and give us a few suggestions based on our results."* He offered his hand to Seth. *"I'll try to come see you next week."*

"Please, reconsider everything we've discussed." Seth gripped Aiden's hand. *"I don't want anything to happen to you."*

As Aidan took a few steps away, Martha embraced her son. Seth whispered something to the old woman, which made her laugh. Still smiling, she hooked her arm through the crook of Aiden's elbow, then together they made their way from the visiting room. Celeste rushed after them.

"What did my dad say to you?" Aiden asked Martha as they neared a black Jeep.

A big grin split Martha's wrinkled face. *"I hope you die."*

Celeste was torn from the parking lot and shoved back to reality. She opened her eyes, and met Martha's gaze. "Why would your own son want you dead?"

Martha smiled and looked to Aiden. "You're right. She is good."

"Amazing. What else did you see?" Aiden asked.

"You and your grandmother planned my kidnapping." She let the watch fall into Aiden's hand. "Your father doesn't want you to do this. Why won't you listen to him and learn from his mistakes?"

Aiden slipped the watch around his wrist. "I was ten when my father was arrested. Do you have any idea what it's like to spend almost your entire life without your father?"

She did. Her mother had married Hugh Risinski prior to her birth. The man had also fathered her sister, Eden, and brother, Will. Hugh, the man who'd raised her, the man she'd called Dad, had been the only father she'd ever known. Ian Scott was her true biological father, her real dad, and she'd spent nearly three decades never knowing he existed.

"What about your mother?" Celeste asked.

He shrugged. "Without a word or note, she left us just before my ninth birthday. I've never heard from her since. She's dead to me."

"Maybe she really is dead. Maybe your father killed her."

"My father would never do such a thing," Aiden said, his tone angry. He picked up the electrodes. "You are never to speak of him in a negative way again. Do you understand?"

"Yes, it won't happen again," she assured him, and when Martha approached with a mouth guard, Celeste clamped her mouth closed and turned her head to the side.

Martha gripped Celeste's jaw. "Open. You don't want to bite off your tongue."

"I'll do another reading." Tears streamed down the sides of Celeste's face and into her hair. Fear gripped her by the throat. "Please don't do this. I've read about electroconvulsive therapy. It's not going to enhance my gift. If anything, it could destroy it, along with some of my memories."

"We're fully aware that people are prone to memory loss after therapy," Aiden said. "*But*, my father gave one of his patients several rounds of electroshock and her abilities weren't just enhanced, they became incredibly powerful. Grandma knows, because she was there and saw what the girl could do with her mind. It was amazing and incredible."

Suspecting Aiden was referring to Karen, Celeste glanced at the ghost. "What happened to her?" she asked.

"When she tried to kill my father, he realized she was too

powerful to control. So he tried to reverse that power by giving her a lobotomy, which she didn't survive." He rested the electrodes against Celeste's temples, while Martha forced the mouth guard between her lips. "Don't look at your therapy as punishment, that's not what this is. We need to gauge what will work on you and what won't, before the final experiment. Electroshock, in my opinion, is safer than pumping your body with mind-altering drugs. Plus, my father proved that therapy *does* enhance certain gifts. We'll want you to give us another reading later. Next time, we're going to ask for specific details of certain events." He smiled. "It's going to be fun."

Panicking, Celeste spat out the mouth guard. "What if I can't? What if none of this works, or *I* become too powerful for you to control?"

Martha pushed the plastic back into Celeste's mouth, then held her by the head and jaw. "I'm a believer in lobotomies."

Celeste's screams were muted by the mouth guard and Martha's grip.

"Don't worry. It shouldn't come to that." Aiden reached for the machine's control panel. "This will only last a second," he said, then flipped a switch.

Pain shot through Celeste's skull. Aiden immediately removed the electrodes from her temples, while Martha continued to hold her head still. A deafening roar muted all other sounds. Her body stiffened and jerked uncontrollably. Her mind went blank. Her vision blurred, her surroundings turned stark white.

A scream sliced through the room. The ghost's aura penetrated the white light, becoming a blinding shade of yellow. The young girl's body swelled, filling up a portion of the room and swallowing the bed and Celeste's legs. When the ghost cried out again, releasing a painful, sad howl, the power died.

Celeste's body slammed against the bed. Involuntarily twitched and jerked. Her heart thumped hard and fast. Bile rose from her throat. Dragging deep breaths through her nose, she bit down on the mouth guard, grunting, crying. Her muscles stiff and burning, as if she'd spent twelve hours at the gym, she couldn't move, couldn't find the energy.

Aiden smoothed damp hair from her forehead, then reached for the switch again. "I wonder if this old thing caused a fuse to blow."

"Better hope that's the case." Martha walked to the dresser, opened a drawer and pulled out a blanket. "If we have to bring in an electrician, we'll need to do something with Celeste and George. Don't forget I have to finish that afghan, and I also have baking to do. I promised to take muffins to the church in the morning."

Hatred for the woman and her grandson burned through Celeste. Over the years, she'd encountered vile people, killers who hadn't valued anyone's life but their own. She'd dealt with wicked ghosts bent on dragging her into their hell. But these people... How could the old woman casually talk about baking and going to church with Celeste bound to the bed, her body still shuddering from the electric jolt to her brain?

While Aiden unplugged the machine and placed it back in the cabinet, Martha removed Celeste's mouth guard, then covered her with the light blanket. "Get some rest. We'll be back in a few hours."

Her mouth dry, her tongue heavy, thick, Celeste couldn't respond. Even if she could, what would she say? There was no talking sense into these people. They truly believed in what they were doing...especially Aiden. The man had misguided beliefs which Celeste suspected were due to not only having Asperger's syndrome, but being raised by his grandmother. Something was off about Martha. Even when she attempted to be sincere and kind, there was a hint of malice lurking in her cold gaze.

Once Aiden and Martha had left the room, closing the door behind them, Celeste lay motionless, helpless...vulnerable. Tears stung her eyes. Exhausted, defeated, she closed them and prayed for sleep...and death.

"You don't want to die." The ghost returned and hovered next

to the bed. *"It's so lonely here. There's no love or light. Just sadness and misery."* She cocked her head and studied Celeste. *"I thought you were Janice. You look so much like your mother. I'm sorry she died."*

Wanting to curl into a ball, but unable to because of the restraints, Celeste cried harder. She didn't want to think about her mom or talk to Karen. Her head hurt, her body ached, and the fear, the utter terror… She couldn't cope with it. Couldn't even picture John or her kids. What if she never saw them again? Kissed her husband, held her babies. "Go away," she said on a sob. "I can't do this right now."

Karen suspended her body over Celeste's. *"But you must. It will only get worse."*

Celeste closed her eyes. "I'd rather die."

"Look at me," Karen said, her voice strong, urgent.

With reluctance, Celeste forced her heavy lids open, and gasped. Karen's white hair was gone, and in its place were blood and crude stitches along the center of her skull.

"You don't want them experimenting on you." The ghost lowered until she was inches from Celeste. *"Let me show you why,"* she said, then entered Celeste's body…

CHAPTER 4

CELESTE SUCKED IN a deep breath the moment Karen's spirit became one with her body. The room tilted, rotated, then was plunged into darkness. Her memories collided with Karen's. Images of John and the kids mingled with a couple she didn't know, and an unfamiliar teen's room coated with posters and objects floating or suspended in the air. Kids she didn't recognize were in her face, making fun of her, shoving her around, calling her names. A man, maybe a minister or priest, came into focus for a brief moment. She was then shoved back into the room where she was being held, her head filling with whispered words that were not her own.

She glanced around her. The room looked different, more clinical, and there were several pieces of equipment she couldn't identify. When she drew in another deep breath and looked down at her body, the blunt edges of long, stark white hair rose along her chest, together with several restraints.

"Keep calm. You're with me now," Karen said. *"My body, my thoughts. You need to see, need to understand why you must fight."*

Celeste froze. Karen had possessed her. Except this wasn't Celeste's body. And if she had somehow entered Karen's, then she was no longer in the present, but the past. The unfamiliar memories, the whispering in her head, must be the girl's. After having just gone through electroconvulsive therapy, and knowing that thirty-five years ago Karen had not only been given the same, but also a lobotomy, Celeste dreaded what was coming next.

The door opened and a younger version of Dr. Ryker entered

the room, looking the part of a surgeon with his white lab coat, gloves and surgical cap. A woman wearing a nurse's uniform also stepped inside. Although the woman had gray streaks running through her dark hair, along with smooth, firm skin, Celeste easily recognized Martha Ryker. Not because of her over-sized glasses, but by the way her blue eyes glittered with wickedness.

Not again, Karen's thoughts whispered through Celeste's mind as if they were her own. *Please, not again.*

"Good morning, Karen," Dr. Ryker began. "How are you feeling today?"

Horrible. I wish you were dead. "My head hurts. And I really miss my family. When can they come visit me?"

Dr. Ryker frowned. "We've been over this before. Your parents do not want to see you until you've been cured."

Liar. They love me. They would never let you hurt me. "Couldn't I at least talk to them on the phone. I need to hear my mom and dad's voices. I promise, I won't say anything about what you're doing to me."

"What I'm doing to you?" Seth shook his head. "Why should I be worried about what you tell your parents? I'm a doctor, you're my patient, and I'm treating you in the best way I see fit."

By electrocuting me? "Do my parents know about the shock therapy?"

"They're fully aware."

Still lying.

"And," he continued, "they've given me permission to do everything in my power to cure you."

"I don't need to be cured. There's nothing wrong with me," Karen said, her voice strong and filled with conviction. "I like myself."

He pulled a metal folding chair next to the bed, then sat. "You're a telepathic and telekinetic albino." His expression turned grave. "I'm sorry, Karen, there is plenty wrong with you. And while I appreciate that you embrace your...abnormalities, your parents feel it's important for you to lead a normal life."

"I'll never be normal. I can't change my skin color. Even if I could, I wouldn't. Being albino doesn't define me, and I don't mind being different. Same goes for my gifts. God gave them to me, why should they be taken away?"

"God allows some children to be born with deformities. Should we not use our medical knowledge to help those children lead normal lives?"

Anger warmed the girl's cheeks, filled her with hatred. "I'm not *deformed*."

"Who's the doctor here?" Martha asked, drawing Karen's attention. "You, or my son?" The nurse narrowed her eyes. "In your current state, you're a dangerous creature who should be locked in a cell until your body expires. No one is safe around you."

That's not true! God, I hate that bitch. "I've never hurt anyone," Karen said with vehemence.

"Not yet." Dr. Ryker touched her arm. "What if, in a fit of rage, you use your mind to throw a steak knife at your mom?"

"I can barely move a playing card across the table," Karen said, but Celeste knew the lie was for self-preservation. She'd glimpsed Karen's memories and had caught a quick image of objects moving around the teen's room.

"There's also the telepathy," Seth continued as if Karen hadn't spoken. "Your parents are concerned about privacy. They don't want you listening to their thoughts and reading their minds."

The girl was suddenly consumed by deep sadness and humiliation. Celeste didn't sense her mood, she *felt* it as if it were hers to own and bear. "I wouldn't dare do that." Karen closed her eyes and, for a brief second, Celeste saw a teenaged boy with dark curly hair and hazel eyes. Then she heard him whisper 'freak' without moving his mouth. "It's better to not know what people truly think of you," Karen said, looking up at the doctor. "It can hurt too much."

"Which is why we need to heal you." Dr. Ryker smiled. "Today, we're going to run a couple of experiments before we give you your therapy. After you've rested, you'll be allowed to visit the communal room for dinner and television. Doesn't that sound nice? Mother says *Who's the Boss?* is on this evening, followed by *Growing Pains* and *Moonlighting*."

Because after tomorrow's surgery, you might not know your name. The doctor's voice filled Karen/Celeste's mind.

Karen's heart rate sped from fear as she glanced to Martha. "I like *Growing Pains*," she said, not looking away from the older woman.

And I want to inflict pain. Martha's thoughts had Karen swallowing hard. "Will we continue therapy tomorrow, too?" she asked Dr. Ryker.

A wry smile tugged at Seth's lips, while his gaze was an odd combination of suspicion and amusement. "Interesting, I was just thinking about tomorrow." He leaned close and gave a lock of Karen's white hair a gentle tug. "You weren't reading my mind, were you?"

"No! I swear."

Lying bitch. Martha's voice streamed through Karen/Celeste's head, along with the doctor's, who also mentally accused the girl of being deceitful.

Don't listen, don't listen, don't listen, Karen told herself, while trying to calm her racing heart and keep her breathing normal. "What experiments will you do today?" she asked.

"I want to monitor your brain activity while having you move an object with your mind. Later, I plan to bring in one of the other patients. I'd like to have you place an image or idea in their mind, then see if they are aware of what you've planted."

I won't be alone. Karen relaxed. While an eerie calm settled over the girl, Celeste knew electroconvulsive therapy was inevitable, and her heart ached for her.

"Which patient?" Karen asked.

Dr. Ryker held up a thin helmet covered in sensors and wires, which looked as if it were a prop from a low budget science fiction movie. He slipped the helmet over Karen's head. "Darla hasn't quite recovered from yesterday's treatment, so Mother and I thought it would be a good idea to use our new patient, Janice. You haven't met her yet, but I think you'll like her."

A barrage of emotions slammed into Celeste. After six years of grieving, today, she would see her mom again. While in the body of a ghost...

Maxine Morehouse's Residence, Chicago, Illinois
Saturday, 12:05 p.m. Central Daylight Time

JOHN KEPT HIS gag reflex in check as he lay Mason on the area rug of Maxine's front parlor. After placing a disposable changing pad beneath his son, he tackled Mason's dirty diaper. He'd come to Maxine's hoping she could help Olivia show him Celeste again. They'd only been there for ten minutes when Mason had decided to do his business. Better now than if Olivia was in the middle of a reading.

He pulled baby wipes from the diaper bag. Was it possible that his three-year-old could do an actual reading? Did he really want that for her? He needed to find Celeste, would give his life to save her, but was worried how a psychic reading would affect Olivia. Especially if she saw her mother being hurt.

John gagged again. "Buddy, you stink." Mason grinned and turned to roll. "Nope, not happening, squirmy worm. Hold still. Daddy's almost done," he said, using a baby wipe to clean his son.

Before he could finish putting Mason in a fresh diaper, his cell phone rang. Holding the clean diaper over him to avoid being peed on, John quickly pulled the phone from his pocket and saw the call came from FBI Agent, Laura Grabowski. He tucked it under his chin. "Hi, Laura," he answered, and continued to fit Mason with the diaper.

"Hey, John. How are you and the kids? I hope you were able to get some sleep."

At around two a.m., after receiving the BOLO from the FBI, an Indiana State Trooper had contacted Agent Grabowski, claiming that at midnight, he'd seen a black Jeep with Pennsylvania plates at a rest area off I-80 East. The trooper said he remembered the Jeep because the passenger, an old woman with snow-white hair, glasses and wearing a red jacket, had him thinking about Christmas in July. And while the Jeep they were looking for had stolen Ohio plates, John, along with the other investigators involved, had decided it was possible the kidnappers had switched out the plates. Fortunately, the trooper had remembered the first three letters on the plate.

After Agent Grabowski had run the partial tag, they'd discovered one with the same registration had been stolen the day before from Clarion, Pennsylvania. Between the Ohio and Pennsylvania plates, along with the Indiana State Trooper's report, they believed the kidnappers were not only from the east, but heading back in that direction as well.

By three a.m., and after being told the only fingerprints on the ice bucket found in the hedges belonged to Celeste, John had decided there wasn't much more they could do from Madison, Wisconsin. While he'd wanted to run the investigation personally, he also needed to take care of Olivia and Mason. Wanting the kids to have some semblance of normalcy, he'd chosen to fly his family home via Ian's jet, while Hudson and Dante had driven his van back to Chicago. By the time he'd gotten home and had got the kids settled, he wasn't sure, but he might have slept for an hour.

"The kids are okay, thanks," John said, snapping Mason's onesie back in place. "Have you heard from the Toledo PD?" When they'd discovered the Ohio plates had been stolen from the parking lot of a Motel 6 just outside of Toledo, Ohio, they'd become concerned that the kidnappers' MO was snatching victims from hotels.

"Yes, it's one of the reasons I'm calling. Toledo PD says they didn't receive any missing persons reports, and that no one staying in the area hotels contacted them with regard to an assault or attempted kidnapping. The detective I spoke with said he went to Motel 6, talked with hotel employees and showed them the photos we have of the man and woman from the surveillance footage. The good news is, several employees remembered the couple. The hotel manager pulled up records and reported that George Meadows and a guest stayed there Thursday night. The employees recognized the old woman, but because the man wore a hat, they couldn't provide a positive ID."

"You've got a name?" John asked, hope working through him.

"Name, address and credit card. The bad news is, the man who the credit card belonged to went missing from his home in North Bethesda, Maryland, three days ago."

Fuck. Why couldn't it be easy?

"That isn't necessarily bad news." John stowed the dirty diaper in a plastic grocery bag, while Mason rolled onto his belly, then scooted into a crawl position. "We know the kidnappers were in Maryland. We need to investigate George Meadows, talk with his family, friends and coworkers. This could be our starting point."

"I considered the same," Laura said. "Which is why I've requested to have several agents look into Meadows' background, and check his house for signs of foul play."

"I can be there in a couple hours."

"No, John." Laura released a sigh. "I'm familiar with your history with the FBI and CORE. You're an excellent investigator, but you're too emotionally connected to this case. That being said, I certainly wouldn't be opposed to you running your own investigation through CORE. I want to find your wife, too, and will take the additional help."

He'd had no intention of waiting for permission to find Celeste, neither had Ian. Even now, Rachel Malcolm, CORE's forensic computer analyst and top researcher, along with other members of their team, were at the office poring over files and looking for who could have been behind Celeste's abduction. At first, John had considered the kidnapping random, until he'd thought about the old woman. While he'd been sitting in the van waiting for Celeste to secure their hotel room, he'd seen the white-haired old lady enter the hotel, then leave minutes later when Celeste exited. She and her accomplice hadn't been spotted roaming any of the other floors, just the one where he, Celeste and the kids had been staying. Which led him to firmly believe Celeste had been targeted.

"Our agents are already investigating my wife's disappearance," he said. "You do realize that the people behind this came after her, correct?"

"We can't confirm that, not yet."

"Laura, we now know they drove from Maryland to Wisconsin. We also know they were last seen driving east."

Laura let out another breath. "As if they picked up their package and were heading home. It's possible. But we can't be sure where home is for them. They could've driven up from Florida, or south from New Hampshire, and as they passed through Maryland, did something to George Meadows, then continued toward Wisconsin. My biggest problem with considering your wife as targeted is that they waited to take her from a hotel. Why not abduct her closer to home? Think about her normal routine. Wouldn't there have been more opportunities for the kidnappers to grab her during a regular day?"

"Maybe they'd planned to, but didn't plan on us going out of town."

"We can speculate all we want, but until we have a few solid leads, that's all we'll be able to do," Laura said, then went on to tell him that forensics investigators had found nothing at the Fairmont Inn in Madison, but that the Toledo PD planned to bring their forensics unit to Motel 6 and search the room the couple had used.

"Thanks for keeping me in the loop." John slung the diaper bag over his shoulder, picked up Mason and the bag with the dirty diaper. "I'm with Ian now, so I'll tell him what we discussed."

"Be sure to let me know if CORE gets any leads. I'll call you later after I hear from our agents in Maryland."

After the call ended, and before he polluted the house, John placed the dirty diaper outside on Maxine's front stoop with the intention of tossing it in her trash cans near the garage when he left. He then carried Mason into Maxine's unicorn room, where Olivia sat on the area rug holding a ball and smiling. Wearing jeans, a T-shirt and his shit-kickers, Hudson looked ridiculous sitting perched on one of Maxine's unicorn upholstered wingback chairs. Ian stood next to the chair. Both men had their gazes locked on Olivia. When John glanced to Maxine and Eden, who sat on the couch and were also staring at his daughter with awe in their eyes, he realized he'd missed something while changing Mason's diaper.

"What's happening?" he asked, sitting on the floor near Olivia.

Ian held up a hand. "Ssh."

"Did you just ssh me?"

"I did," Ian said. "Watch." His father-in-law nodded to Olivia. "Go ahead, do it again."

Grinning, Liv looked toward the unlit fireplace and rolled the ball. It came to an abrupt halt before reaching the hearth, then was pushed forward. Rolled along the area rug and landed in his daughter's open hands.

As Mason grunted and reached toward his sister, a shiver ran up John's spine. "Liv? Are you playing catch with someone?"

Olivia bobbed her head. "Edwart. He Mommy an Aunt Maxie's friend."

Edward. The ghost who resided at Maxine's. Fucking great. His kid was playing ball with a dead guy. "You can see Edward?" he asked, wondering if Celeste had known. And if she had, why hadn't she told him?

"Mmm-hmm." Olivia rolled the ball again. "An Edwart's friends."

John didn't look around the room, but noticed everyone except Maxine did. "How many friends?"

"Um, I fink sixty-ninety hundred." Olivia giggled. "Edwart say ten," she amended, holding up five fingers.

"There are ten ghosts in the room?" Hudson leaned his large frame into the petite chair and looked to Maxine. "How can you live here?"

"Unlike the spiritual residents of your previous home," Maxine began, "my ghosts adore me and would never do me any harm. They are, after all, my family."

Hudson frowned. "Yeah, but don't you worry about them watching you when you're in the bathroom or...never mind," he said, when his wife, Eden, cleared her throat.

Olivia grabbed herself by the waist, bent forward and let out a deep belly laugh. After a moment, she looked to Hudson. "Edwart say he not like stinky potty," she said with a giggle, and pinched her nose.

"My potty...bathroom does not stink," Maxine said, her tone defensive. "Edward, no more games. Olivia has to work now."

Olivia held the ball still. "He say okay. Him wanna find Mommy with Livy and Daddy."

"Very good." Maxine smiled. "Honey, do you remember how you held your daddy's hand and showed him Mommy?"

Liv's lower lip shot out in a disgruntled pout and she crossed her arms over her chest. "I try again. It no work."

"That's okay," Maxine assured her. "I have something I'd like you to do. It could help you see your mommy again."

"Don't tell her that," John said when Olivia brightened. "I don't want her disappointed if this doesn't work." Or if he couldn't find Celeste. He quickly pushed the thought from his mind. He needed to stay positive for his kids and his own sanity.

"Of course." Maxine's eyes held apology. "Did you bring her crayons?"

John reached inside the diaper bag and pulled out a pad of paper and crayons. "What works for Celeste might not work for Liv. What then?"

"Let's worry about that if the time comes." Maxine smiled at Olivia. "Would you like to play a game with Aunt Maxie."

Olivia shook her head. "I want Mommy."

"I know, sweetie. And this game is going to help us maybe find your mommy. Okay?" Maxine rose from the sofa to sit next to Olivia on the floor. She took the paper and crayons from John, then placed them in front of the little girl. "Since I know your favorite color is purple, we'll use this crayon." She placed the crayon in Olivia's hand. "Can you color with your eyes closed?"

Olivia scrunched her face and squeezed her eyes tightly, and let Maxine lead her hand to the pad of paper. "It hard," Olivia said with another giggle.

"I know it is, but this is what your mommy does when she wants to see certain things. Here, let Aunt Maxie help you." Maxine guided Olivia's hand, creating a figure eight. Together, they drew another on top of the original, then another, until the purple eight became thick and bold. "Without looking, do you know what we're drawing?"

Olivia shook her head.

"Squeeze your eyes and pretend you can see your hand coloring. Think very hard and tell me what you see."

Olivia gasped. "A snowman!"

"Very good. Now open your eyes and watch your hand making the snowman." When Olivia did, Maxine said, "Keep watching, keep thinking about the snowman and your mommy."

Mason stilled in John's arms. The room became incredibly quiet. Olivia did as Maxine instructed and never took her gaze off the paper or crayon.

"What's the purple doing?" Maxine finally asked.

"Make hole."

The vortex. John had seen it when his daughter had taken his hand at the hotel. Celeste had also once told him that when performing a reading, she felt as if she were freefalling into a whirling tunnel, and at the end of that tunnel was a small opening leading her to another time and place. "Olivia, stop," he said, panicking, fearing where his daughter would go alone and what she might see.

Instead of obeying, Olivia drew faster. "Look, Daddy. I make big hole."

John stood and handed Mason to Eden. He knelt next to

Olivia. "Honey, Daddy doesn't want you going into the hole. You're not big enough yet to go by yourself."

"Let her be," Ian said. "We need her help."

"We don't. I just spoke with Laura. They have a few leads."

"But they don't have Celeste. I want my daughter back."

"And I don't want to lose mine in the process," John argued.

Olivia looked up from the paper and around the room. "My belly hurt." She lifted the crayon and started making circles in the air with it. "Aunt Maxie's ponies flying."

"It's the tunnel," Maxine whispered to John. "The room must be spinning, giving her the impression my unicorn figurines are moving. Has Celeste told you about the tunnel?"

He nodded. "I know what she sees in the vortex. And I don't want Liv going there. How will she know to come back? What if there's something on the other side that has sinister intentions," he said, thinking of Vigo. He knew that during a regular reading Celeste couldn't interact with the people she saw, but was there as an invisible bystander. Still, Olivia was young, impressionable and, unlike her mother, she didn't know how to control her gift.

"I hadn't thought of that." Maxine frowned. "What if I attempt to go with her?" she asked, taking Olivia's free hand. "If she was able to show you Celeste through touch, maybe she can show me, too. When we're through, I can lead her back to you."

Olivia closed her eyes and continued to draw circles in the air. Her forehead puckered. "I go with Daddy." She opened her eyes and stared at Maxine with accusation. "Aunt Maxie gots secret," she said pulling her hand away and reaching for John. "Her tell fib. That not good. Liv no tell fib."

John brushed her curls with his knuckles. "No. You're a good girl," he said, wondering what the hell was up with Olivia, accusing both Maxine and Ian of having secrets. When he'd asked Ian about what Liv had said at the hotel, his father-in-law had shrugged it off, saying he had no idea why she would say such a thing. Suspicious by nature, John wanted to know their secrets, especially if it had something to do with his wife or children.

Olivia smiled. "Daddy see ponies fly?"

"I don't."

She squeezed his hand tightly, and stopped making circles with the crayon. "I scared," she whispered.

"Why, honey? Daddy's with you."

Olivia shook her arm. "Livy purple."

"The vortex is reaching for her," Maxine said. "Olivia, it's okay. The purple won't hurt you. Show Daddy what you see."

His stomach tightening with dread and indecision, John wanted to scoop up his daughter, grab his son and run. Olivia was too little to understand the power her tiny body contained, and it scared the hell out of him. He didn't want her scarred, didn't want her fearing the gift that would follow her through life.

"All will be fine, Miss Olivia," a man with a clipped, English accent assured her. *"We will not allow anything to happen to you."*

Out of the corner of John's eye, shadows shaped in human form moved around the room and toward his daughter. Logic told him to take the kids out of here. But since meeting Celeste, he'd learned there was more to life than logic, science and evidence. There was another realm, a bend between the past, present and future he hadn't considered possible. And as the shadows took shape, revealing facial features, expressions of concern and clothes, he knew now was one of those times where he had to set the rational side of him aside and simply believe in the impossible.

"Edwart," Olivia murmured, and reached out her hand.

A man wearing a black tailcoat, bow tie and carrying a top hat approached Olivia, and held a hand in front of the one she used to create circles. Beneath his thick mustache, his mouth slid into a smile. *"Remember, my dear, this is a safe place."* He looked to John and gave him a single nod. *"Mr. Kain, so nice to finally meet you. Allow me to introduce myself. I'm Edward Robert Morehouse, Maxine's great-great uncle."* He motioned behind him toward the other ghosts. Men and women of various ages and dressed in clothes from several different eras moved closer to John and Olivia, surrounding them and creating a circle. *"We adore your wife and* children." Edward's smile grew. *"You're a lucky fellow. I was terribly frightened for you when Vigo invaded your body."*

"Thank you for helping me." John looked to the other ghosts. "Thank you," he repeated, his throat tightening. He'd been to the other side, and it saddened him that these people chose to remain here instead of basking in the warmth and love the light held.

"You weren't meant to be among us," Edward said, spreading his arms. *"And we are a family. There is much warmth and love here."* He knelt in front of Olivia. *"Show your father the purple along your arm."*

"I scared."

"You will be safe. Show him."

Olivia squeezed John's hand tighter, closed her eyes and rotated her arm faster. "See, Daddy?"

Thick bands of purple hugged her hand and forearm, while rope-like strips splintered from the bands, stretching toward her shoulder and waist. "I see it," John said, amazed by what was happening, and wondering if Celeste experienced the same when she performed a reading.

"John," Edward began, *"place your hand over Miss Olivia's, and let her gift wrap itself around you. So long as you stay connected, you will see what she sees."*

"How do you know?" John was still worried about his daughter, how this vision would affect her, and uncertain if he could even navigate in the psychic world.

"Celeste often uses your image and her love for you to keep her grounded to your world. Miss Olivia, though a small child, does much the same." Edward smiled, and stared at Olivia. *"Such a precious child. Without knowing it, she projects her thoughts. Her love for life, for you, Celeste and Mason, is extremely powerful. Trust in that love."* He shifted his ghostly gaze to John. *"And go find your wife."*

Determined to do just that, and although not quite confident about joining Olivia in a vision, John knelt and, hugging her from behind, rested his arm along hers. The purple bands once again split, then wrapped around his hand and wrist. There was a tug, but not to his arm. Instead, it was as if he were being pulled from inside the center of his body. The room began to spin. All around him, unicorn figurines moved as if they were actually flying.

"I see the ponies now," he whispered in Olivia's ear, and helped her to continue to create the figure eight in the air.

"Daddy see hole?"

John looked ahead. The flying unicorns and purple bands rotated faster, creating a swirling tunnel which narrowed in the distance. A bright light pierced the vortex, called to him. "I see it, honey. We need to go there, okay?"

"An find Mommy."

"Right, and find Mommy. Can you do that? Can you take us there?"

"Olivia, what does your Mommy look like?" Edward asked, his voice tinny, far away.

"She haf yellow hair. Blue eyes…"

A force propelled John forward. Hanging onto his daughter's hand, his stomach dropping as if he were on a roller coaster, he fought from becoming sick. The rotating unicorns and purple bands made him dizzy. Concentrating on the center of the vortex, on his wife, John kept his gaze locked on the white light. The hole grew wider, and wider still, until he and Olivia were thrust through the portal.

"Purple all gone." Olivia raised their joined arms, and held his hand. She looked around her. "Where Mommy?"

"I don't know," John said, wondering whose house they were in, and if this was where Celeste was being held.

"John," Maxine called. *"Can you hear me?"*

"Yes," he replied, his gaze touching on an antique lamp resting on an end table covered in a white doily. A grandfather clock stood against one wall, the time reading twelve-twenty. In another room the theme song from the old television show, *Gunsmoke,* played.

"Do you know where you are?"

"A house. I don't know whose, and I'm not even sure of the

time period." As far as he knew, Celeste's visions were of the past. Yet, at the hotel, Olivia had showed him her mother in the present. That was what he wanted to see. He needed to know Celeste was okay, that they hadn't hurt her.

He needed to see the faces of the kidnappers.

"Can you walk through the house?" Maxine asked.

Still holding Olivia's hand, he started for the room where the TV was located. "We're on the move," he said, stopping at the room's entrance. A flat screen television hung on the wall near the fireplace. A gently rocking dark-green recliner faced the TV. Each time the chair moved, it revealed the top of a snow-white head.

"We might have something," he whispered, then remembered he was now like Celeste, an invisible bystander. He led Olivia into the room. As they neared the chair, a man with light brown hair, blue eyes and a medium build entered from another room.

"Timer buzzed," the man said, dropping onto a dark-green and white plaid sofa. "If you didn't have the TV so loud you could've heard it."

"Did you pull out the muffins?" a woman asked.

"Yeah, they're on top of the stove. They smell good."

"Did you check on the girl?"

"She's sleeping. It's weird. She's sleeping with her eyes open."

John walked Olivia closer to the chair, then stopped and stared at the old woman he recognized from the video surveillance. Though eager to search the house for Celeste, he couldn't help his wife if he didn't know where they were.

"Miss Santa Claus," Olivia began, "where Mommy?"

His throat tightened. Olivia was too young, too innocent to begin to comprehend where they were and that these were *not* good people. "Honey, she can't hear you. And she's not Santa's wife," he added, not wanting Olivia to fear St. Nick.

"Her eyes open?" The old woman frowned as she continued to knit a blanket. "You're sure she's not dead or in a coma."

"She has a pulse and is breathing." He toed off his shoes, then laid on the sofa. "I'm beat from all the driving I did last night. I wouldn't mind getting in a nap before dinner. What time are we eating?"

"I thought we'd eat around four-thirty. That way we can get her testing done early. And tomorrow, I need to be at First Baptist by nine, so I'd like to be in bed on good time. I'm tired, too."

"I don't know from what," the man replied as he rested his head against a throw pillow. "I'm the one who drove."

"I offered to drive."

The man chuckled. "You haven't had a license in six years." He let out a sigh and covered his eyes with the crook of his arm. "Which means I'll have to be up early to take you to church."

"Didn't I tell you Phyllis is taking me?"

The man yawned. "She is? Good. I'm not comfortable leaving those two here alone."

"I'm not, either. George isn't right in the head. I don't trust him." She set her knitting supplies aside, then pushed herself out of the recliner. "I'll go check on the girl. I don't like that she's sleeping with her eyes open. Something could be wrong."

"I think she's fine." The man lifted his arm and looked up at the old woman. "And I don't like you going up and down the basement steps without me. They're too steep and narrow. Give me a sec and I'll go with you."

"I'm quite capable, thank you."

"Grandma, don't argue with me. Look what happened to Mrs. Smith after she broke her hip last year."

The woman slipped off her glasses. Her mouth slid into a grim line. "She never made it out of that rehab facility." She nodded. "You're right. I'll wait for you. Go ahead and nap. I'm going to start dinner."

"She a gramma," Olivia said as she and John followed the woman into the kitchen.

"That's right." John stopped. There were two doors in the kitchen. One led to the backyard, the other was closed. Wondering if the closed door led to the basement, he reached for the knob and grasped air. "Liv, trying opening the door." Since he wasn't psychic and only along for the ride, maybe she could do it.

When her hand fell through the doorknob, she gasped. Eyes wide, she looked from her hand to him. "I scared," she said, her voice laced with worry. "I gotta potty."

Damn it. He wasn't ready to leave here yet. The little bits of information weren't enough to give them a solid lead. "Don't be scared. That's a little trick Mommy can do, too."

"I want Mommy," she cried, big tears slipping down her cheek. "Hafta go potty." She shifted her feet, then crossed her legs. "Go Aunt Maxie's."

"We will. Just give Daddy another minute," he said, trying to hang onto his patience.

Olivia pulled at his hand and cried harder, louder. Worried what would happen once their hands were no longer joined, he tightened his hold on her and quickly looked around the outdated kitchen for clues that might lead to the identity of the kidnappers. There was a window above the kitchen sink. A calendar hung from a magnet on the refrigerator. Through an open doorway near the oven, he saw a stack of mail sitting on the dining room table. If he could get to the mail, he'd have an address.

"Come on, honey," he said, moving them toward the dining room.

"Mommy!" Olivia wailed, then went boneless. As she dropped to the floor his grip on her loosened. "Go bye-bye!"

"John, what's happening?" Maxine asked, urgency in her voice. *"Come back. I'm worried about Olivia."*

"I just need a sec," he said, kneeling next to his daughter. "Please, baby, give Daddy one more minute. Be a good girl and cooperate."

Olivia stopped bawling and stared ahead. John looked up just as the old woman wrapped her hand around the closed door. The woman glanced over her shoulder to where her grandson slept, then opened the door. The hinges creaked. She looked back again before flipping on a light switch and stepping into the shadowy stairwell.

As the door slowly closed behind her, Olivia stood. "Mommy!" She sprang forward, tearing her hand from his.

"No," John shouted, and lunged for his daughter. When he pulled her small body against his, a massive blast of ice-cold air forced them backward. Clutching Olivia to him, he fell. Before connecting with the floor, they were shoved from the room into a purple abyss, then back inside Maxine's unicorn parlor.

Crying, Olivia curled into him. "Ssh, Daddy's here. I've got you."

"The gramma...she bad. She bad girl," Olivia hiccupped, and started crying again.

John caught one of her tears with his finger. "How do you know?"

She shrugged. "Her bad."

Eden gave Mason to Maxine, moved off the couch and reached her hand toward Olivia. "Come on, sweetie. Auntie E will take you to the bathroom."

With a nod, Olivia took her aunt's hand. Once the two had left the room, John pushed a hand through his hair. When he glanced around and caught Mason staring at him, guilt and disappointment wrapped around his heart. His boy wanted his mommy, and John hadn't delivered.

John looked up at Maxine, and met her concerned gaze. "We were so close," he said, then explained to everyone not only what he'd seen at the house, but what Agent Laura Grabowski had told him earlier.

"This is good." Ian nodded. "Because we know George Meadows went missing in North Bethesda, Maryland, and the couple has a man named George at the house. I think we should start our search in Maryland. I'll contact Rachel and have her look up any churches named First Baptist. The name Smith is common, but we know she died within the past year, and she was likely elderly. An obituary might help us narrow our search down to a specific city."

"They didn't say Mrs. Smith died," John corrected him.

"They said she didn't make it out of the rehab facility. It could be she's still there. But I don't think it would hurt to try. And we do know the woman has a friend named Phyllis."

Hudson rose from the wingback chair. "Once we locate the churches, we could get a list of parishioners and look for Phyllis." He let out a sigh. "I wish we had a better picture of the old lady we could flash around during Sunday services."

John pushed himself off the floor. "I wish we knew *why* they took Celeste." He took Mason from Maxine. "I've dealt with plenty of criminals, but these two don't make sense to me. The woman is old. I'm thinking she's in her eighties. What would motivate her to take part in a kidnapping?"

"You," Ian said, leaning against the fireplace mantel. "If they targeted Celeste, this could boil down to revenge over someone you've arrested."

"Is no one considering that these people will contact John with ransom demands?" Maxine asked.

Ian shook his head. "Kidnappings for ransom are rare. The logistics of safely getting the ransom money without incident would put the abductors at risk. Making money by robbing a bank would be easier than having to hold a person hostage and deal with negotiators."

"I agree with Ian," John said. "I'm also concerned revenge could be their motivation. But it might not be revenge against me." He looked at his father-in-law. "Celeste *is* your only daughter."

Ian rubbed the back of his neck. "I've considered that possibility, too. With how many enemies I've made, and the number of men and women I've helped put in prison, I wouldn't even know where to begin looking for a viable suspect." He shoved his hands in his front pockets. "Which is why I think we should have Olivia perform another reading."

"It's too soon," Maxine protested. "Give her time to recover. You don't want her to fear her gift."

"But she can take John to where my daughter is being held,"

Ian argued.

"Next time, she might go to a different place," Maxine countered, and looked to John. "I didn't ask…do you think what you witnessed was happening in the present?"

"There was a grandfather clock set an hour ahead of us, but if they're on the east coast, that makes sense. Given how the man talked about being tired from the drive, discussing dinner and church tomorrow, I definitely believe we were watching everything as it was happening."

Maxine's brow creased. "That's amazing. Celeste has only been able to do that once, correct?"

John recalled what his wife had told him after she'd found Dante's missing daughter. "Yes, just that one time, as far as I know."

"Well, I suggest we have Olivia perform another reading in the morning. Now that you've been to their house, you can go immediately to the stack of mail on the dining room table."

That was his plan, but he had no intention of waiting until the morning. While the couple had made no indication they would harm Celeste, or that they thought she'd be dead by the morning, shit happened. He also hadn't liked the way the old lady had snuck into the basement, or how the man had found Celeste sleeping with her eyes open. In all the years he'd known Celeste, the only time she'd been in a catatonic state with her eyes open, was when she'd been in a trance. And if that were the case here, where had his wife gone this time?

Hating the helplessness and fear suffocating him, he gathered Mason's diaper bag. "I don't want to wait until the morning. I'd like to bring Liv back after dinner."

Maxine shook her head. "I wouldn't advise that, John. Again, you don't want her to come to fear her gift."

"I heard you the first time," he said, not hiding his frustration. "But she's my daughter. If you won't help us—"

"Of course I'll help you. Please understand that I'm not trying to prevent you from finding Celeste. I love your wife and want her home. But Olivia is young. She doesn't understand the things she's seeing and can't comprehend her abilities. I don't want one of her last images of her mother to be..." She let out a shaky breath. "We just don't know what these people plan to do to Celeste."

John understood all of this and also wanted to keep his daughter protected from any possible outcome. Except time wasn't on their side. The first twenty-four hours of abduction cases were the most critical. After that, every passing hour lessened the chances of finding the victim. By day three, the hope of discovering the victim alive and unharmed, diminished. And Celeste had been taken approximately seventeen hours ago.

"Let's give Rachel a couple hours to research the leads John gave us," Ian suggested. "Maybe we won't need to use Olivia. I'm also anxious to hear what the FBI finds when they further investigate George Meadows' disappearance."

"Please, John," Maxine began, "listen to Ian on this. In the morning, if we're nowhere closer to finding Celeste, we can have Olivia perform another reading."

"Fine. One more thing before we go..." John slung the diaper bag over his shoulder and looked from Ian to Maxine. "Last night Olivia said Ian had a secret. Today, she claims you do, too. Is there something you two aren't telling me?"

Maxine frowned. "Secret? That's strange." She faced Ian. "I have no clue, do you?"

Ian nodded. "Yes, Olivia's three," he said as if her young age was all the explanation needed.

"And psychic," Hudson added with a shrug. "That's quite the combo. I'd want to know what secret she saw, too. But I'm nosey and suspicious by nature."

Ian's jaw hardened. Before he could say anything more on the subject, Olivia came back into the room with Eden. His daughter looked up at John, purple smudges underscoring her eyes. "Daddy, I tired," she said, taking his hand.

After saying goodbye to the others, John placed the kids in the van and left. When they reached their house, he gathered them and headed inside. "How about a snack, then a nap?" he asked Olivia, once he had Mason in his crib.

She yawned and nodded. "Haf apple for snack?"

While he pulled the apple from the fridge, Olivia sat at the table, leafing through a picture book. As John sliced the apple, he couldn't shake *the secret*. He didn't buy Ian's explanation, and thought it strange that Olivia would comment on both Maxine and Ian. Like Hudson, John was also nosey and weighed heavily on the suspicious side.

He set the bowl of apple slices in front of his daughter. "Liv, what is Aunt Maxie's secret? Is it the same as Grandpa Ian's?"

She nodded, then picked up an apple slice and took a bite.

"Liv, honey, tell Daddy. You won't be in trouble if you do."

As Olivia looked down at the bowl of apples, a familiar name filled John's head…

Janice.

CHAPTER 5

The Ryker Residence, Silver Spring, Maryland
Saturday, 2:32 p.m. Eastern Daylight Time

CELESTE'S HEAD POUNDED with exhaustion. Not *her* head, but Karen's, the albino teenager who'd been subjected to grueling hours of experiments. But Karen's aches and pains, her thoughts and that of the others in the room, were now Celeste's. There were so many voices bouncing around in Celeste's head, she was having a difficult time keeping her own thoughts, her fears, straight.

Being able to experience both the physical and mental state of another person wasn't something she wanted to ever go through again. Now she had a good idea of what it had been like for John when he'd been possessed by Vigo. Except John hadn't been able to feel Vigo's pain. When Karen had failed an experiment, Dr. Ryker had zapped her arms, legs or torso with a cattle prod. While the prod had been nothing in comparison to electroconvulsive therapy, after nearly a dozen shocks, the girl's body had hurt all over.

"Come on, Karen," Dr. Ryker said with impatience. "I know you can move the pencil. Make it roll."

Don't think about the pencil. Don't think about the pencil....

During however long Karen had been strapped to the table and wearing the sensor helmet—which fit too tightly and weighed a ton—Dr. Ryker had insisted she move various objects. Each time, Karen would tell herself not to think about those objects. And each time, the items remained inert, which didn't surprise

Celeste. In her experience, telekinesis or mind movement wasn't an ability living humans possessed. Ghosts were different. They existed in a different realm, and she'd witnessed plenty of spirits make objects move without touching them.

"I can't," Karen said, her gaze shifting to the six-inch cattle prod he held. "I'm trying, but I can't make it move. Please don't use that thing on me. Maybe you cured me."

Dr. Ryker smiled and set the prod on a table holding medical tools and various machines, one of which was similar to the old electroshock therapy device Aiden had used on Celeste. "Or maybe you've been repressing." He held up a long narrow strip of paper attached to one of the other machines that reminded Celeste of an old analog polygraph. Along the graph, there were several series of thick spikes, followed by smaller ones. "Science doesn't lie. Every time I've asked you to move an object, we see a rise in brain activity. This leads me to conclude that you're fighting to *not* do as you're told."

"That's not true. I swear," Karen said with desperation. "Please. I'm cured. I've lost my gift."

Dr. Ryker let out an impatient breath and dropped the paper. "I'm not a fool. Don't insult my intelligence."

"I told you to take extreme measures," Martha said. "She's been stringing you along for the past week. The girl can do it. Just tell her the truth."

"The truth?"

"Enough, Mother." Dr. Ryker glared at Martha. "We'll discuss this later. For now, we'll move on to the next experiment. Go get Janice."

At the mention of Celeste's mother's name, nervous energy moved through the girl's body, along with fear. Karen didn't want to be alone with Martha and Dr. Ryker, but was also afraid of what the doctor and nurse team might do to her and Janice. Celeste worried, too. Except, she knew for a fact her mother had left Dr. Ryker's unscathed. According to her mother's journals and Ian's case report, the FBI had stopped Dr. Ryker before he'd had the chance to harm her.

"I'm not your employee." Martha folded her arms across her chest. "You get her."

Without another word, Dr. Ryker left the room. Once the door clicked shut, Martha leaned close to Karen. "I'm glad you didn't do what you were told."

Karen's heart raced, and the girl's hatred blossomed. "Why?"

Martha punched the girl in the stomach. "Because now the fun can finally begin." Celeste felt the girl's pain as Martha hit her again, knocking the breath from Karen's lungs.

Not again, the girl's thoughts penetrated Celeste's. *Stop. Please. No more.* "Please," Karen begged, once she caught her breath.

Martha cupped her ear. "Was that you asking me for more? You've got it," she said, then hit her again. As Karen dragged in deep breaths, Martha placed her hands on either side of the teen's face, then leaned in until their noses almost touched. "I don't know who's crazier…you, your parents or my son. And I know crazy." She smiled. "I don't believe you can move things with your mind or read my thoughts. Fortunately, Seth does. Otherwise retirement would be boring."

Pain radiated from just about every part of Karen's body. The need to curl into a ball, to ward off another blow was strong, not only for Celeste, but Karen, too. The girl ached, cried. Tears coated her face. Karen's mind raced with so much fear it broke Celeste's heart. She wished they could communicate here and now, not just in Celeste's own time. She wanted to console Karen.

The small, wiry, but surprisingly strong woman stepped away from the bed. "Stop your crying and pull yourself together before Seth returns." Martha adjusted the blanket over the girl's body. "By the by, if I'm wrong, and you can do things with your mind, don't you dare plant any ideas in my son's head. If you try to get him to betray me, I will kill you. Not quickly, either."

Martha lifted a pitcher, then filled a glass with water, which she brought over to Karen, and held the straw to the girl's mouth. When Dr. Ryker stepped in the room, it probably looked as if his mother was taking care of his patient, not beating and threatening her.

"Are we restraining Janice?" Martha asked, pulling the straw away, and blocking the view of the door.

"That won't be necessary." Celeste's mother's voice washed over her, along with both sadness and joy. Celeste had hoped to eventually connect with her mom in the spirit realm, but as herself, not an abused stranger. "What do you need me to do?" Janice asked.

"We'll bind her hands and ankles," Dr. Ryker said. "She can sit on a folding chair."

"You don't need to do that," Janice said with vehemence. "Seth, you *know* me."

"I do. I also know of your relationship with Ian Scott. Are you aware Agent Hugh Risinski is also enamored by you?" The doctor chuckled. "I foresee quite the love triangle, and I'm not psychic. That being said, because you likely have *two* FBI agents in love with you, I will defer to my mother on this. Except, I don't think it's necessary to bind your ankles. You're not going anywhere."

Martha finally moved. Grief slammed into Celeste as she stared at her mother. At twenty-six, Janice was thin, young and pretty. Her long curly blond hair draped over her shoulders. Her blue eyes, so much like Celeste and Olivia's, held contempt and fear. The last time Celeste had seen her mother alive, she'd been bald from chemotherapy, bloated from steroids and doped up on morphine to combat the pain. But before her mother's deathbed image could take root, Karen's manic thoughts pushed their way front and center. Relief, terror and deep melancholy collided and circled through the girl's head, until they became jumbled and indiscernible.

To keep her own thoughts clear, Celeste focused on her mother, who was now seated on a metal folding chair near the machine Dr. Ryker used to measure Karen's brain waves. While Martha wrapped electrical tape around Janice's joined wrists and ankles, Dr. Ryker took another of his sensor helmets from the metal cabinet.

"Janice, I'd like you to meet Karen. You two will be working together on a few experiments." He placed the helmet on Janice's head. "And this will allow me to monitor your brain activity," he said, turning on the device. "Here's how it will work. I'll tell Karen what image or thought I want her to plant in your mind. And all you have to do is relay what it is, understand?"

"Telepathy isn't a real thing," Janice said.

Dr. Ryker chuckled. "It's amusing that a psychic who claims to communicate with the dead is skeptical about telepathy. Tell me, what are your thoughts on telekinesis?"

"I have none."

"Interesting. You don't believe mind-movement is possible?"

"Maybe in a Stephen King novel, but not in real life," Janice said, but Celeste sensed her mother was lying. As did Karen.

She believes. I wish she didn't. I wish they'd never brought her here. Karen's worried thoughts rushed through her head. Yes, this wasn't a good situation, and Celeste knew the girl would eventually die here. But Celeste couldn't understand why Karen was afraid for Janice. If anyone should be scared, it should be Karen. For whatever reason, Dr. Ryker was convinced the girl had superhero-like powers. Even worse, the man's mother was violent and cruel. Celeste also wasn't sure why the girl's ghost still haunted this house. Dr. Ryker was serving a life sentence for his crimes against her and the others he'd killed in the name of science.

"Today, I'm going to prove to you that telepathy is indeed very real."

"And telekinesis?" Janice asked. "Will you prove that as well, and at this girl's expense? Seth, you've worked with the FBI, you've been a trusted advisor to agents during several criminal investigations. You have a thriving practice. You have to know what you're doing here is wrong."

"What I'm doing will eventually save lives."

"How?" Janice shook her head. "That makes no sense to me. You're not trying to come up with a cure for cancer, you're playing with peoples' minds."

"How?" Dr. Ryker repeated. "On the battlefield. That's how. When we were in Vietnam, wouldn't it have been fantastic if we'd had an army of super-soldiers? Men and women who could fight with their minds, rather than with guns and bombs? Think about it, Janice. Someone like Karen could have planted our ideologies into the minds of the Vietcong and ended the war before it began. Better yet, she could've used her gift to cause enemy pilots to crash."

"With telekinesis? That's ridiculous."

"Not really. Just a few years ago, the Chinese ran experiments using children thought to have telekinetic abilities. Using only their minds, those children were able to move small objects, not only through physical barriers but they made them float on the air." Dr. Ryker's tone, along with the look on his face, became condescending. "You also can't deny the number of people who've demonstrated that they can bend utensils without touching them."

"Obviously we're not going to agree on this topic," Janice said. "I also hope you understand that even if you can prove people have these abilities, you'll still go to prison for what you've done here."

"Not a chance. The military will want my knowledge and wouldn't let that happen." He walked over to the bed. "Enough about that for now. Karen will need to rest soon, so let's begin." Dr. Ryker leaned in and whispered, "Ladybug," into Karen's ear. He straightened. "Now, Karen, I want you to plant that image or word into Janice's mind."

"I told you, I can't," the girl whined.

He picked up the cattle prod. "Should I give you a reason to cooperate? Or maybe we should go ahead with your electroshock therapy, then revisit this experiment again later today."

"No!" Karen's body stiffened and her heart pounded with panic. "Please don't. I'll try, but I can't guarantee it'll work."

"Electroshock?" Her mother's face twisted with confusion and worry as she looked to Karen. "Seth, you can't be serious. That's barbaric."

"Do you have a medical degree?" he asked with heavy sarcasm. "Of course you don't. Let me explain something to you. Electroshock treatment is similar to using a defibrillator on a person suffering from a heart attack. Shock therapy changes the brain's chemistry and gives it a quick jumpstart. I've given many of my mentally ill patients this type of treatment." He touched Karen's arm. "And, according to her parents, Karen is my patient."

"What mental illness does this young girl suffer?" Janice asked.

"None. She has abilities her parents don't understand. They want them gone, but I want to *enhance* her gift. I want to find out how it works, then how I can take a normal person and make them into a super-soldier."

Betrayal hit Karen with a crushing blow. "You lied."

Martha cleared her throat. "Seth, maybe we should end this session now. Aiden will be home from school soon."

"You *lied*," Karen repeated, louder, stronger. The machine measuring her brain waves moved quickly. "You told me once I was cured, I could go home. Even though I knew it was a lie, I've been telling myself to keep believing anyway."

"How did you know?" Dr. Ryker asked.

"Remember the day your son came in the room after my *therapy*? I'd asked when I could see my parents, and you told me to read your mind for the answer. Do you remember that? Do you remember what you thought?"

Dr. Ryker smiled. "Never."

"Seth, stop this," Janice shouted. "Leave the girl alone. She doesn't have *special powers*. She's a confused kid and clearly her parents—"

"I'm not *confused*." As Karen concentrated on Janice, Celeste saw an image of a ladybug in her mind. "Tell them what you see."

"I don't see anything but a man who needs to be locked behind bars."

"Tell them!" Karen's breathing became labored. Energy, unlike anything Celeste had experienced before, pulled from her core then splintered to every part of her body, giving her a sense of weightlessness. As if gravity didn't exist and the only thing keeping her grounded were the restraints around Karen's body. "Tell them, Janice," Karen demanded, the image of the ladybug growing bolder, brighter.

Janice's eyes filled with tears. *"Don't do this,"* she said, her voice filling Karen's head.

Stunned, Celeste stared at her mother. No. There was no way her mom had been telepathic. Celeste had to have imagined what she'd just heard, or confused her mom's voice for Karen's. Her mom had never mentioned telepathy in her journals, and had never once spoken to Celeste with her mind.

The monitor attached to Janice's brain sensors also began to spike. A tear slipped down her cheek. "Ladybug."

"Outstanding," Dr. Ryker said. "I knew it. Excellent work, Karen. Now I'll give you another image."

"No." The energy humming through the girl's body intensified, became dark as her thoughts turned violent. The girl pictured Dr. Ryker dead. Imagined beating Martha. Saw herself burning down her family's home. "Can you see that?" she asked, turning her head slightly to meet the doctor's gaze.

Amusement made his eyes glitter. "What I see is a super-soldier in the making."

"No," Janice yelled. "Karen, that's not the real you. You wouldn't hurt anyone. You're a kind, gentle soul."

"Mother, silence Janice."

"Seth." Martha tore a wide piece of tape from a roll. "I think you should stop for the day. The girl needs her rest."

"Don't tell me my business." Dr. Ryker glared at his mother. "When you're finished sealing Janice's mouth shut, remove her sensors."

As Martha obeyed her son, Celeste wondered what had gotten into the woman. She'd gone from cruel to concerned since Janice had entered the room, which made little sense.

Dr. Ryker also removed the sensor helmet from Karen's head,

then smoothed her damp hair from her forehead. "You have a very vivid and violent imagination." He took a step back, only to return with electrodes similar to the ones Aiden had used on Celeste earlier. "While I appreciate your inventiveness, I didn't care for the way you depicted Mother and me." He glanced over his shoulder to Martha. "Turn on the machine."

Janice grunted and rose from the metal chair.

"Shove her down." Dr. Ryker's command had Martha moving quickly and forcing Janice back onto the chair. He pointed the electrode at Celeste's mother. "Get up again and your shock therapy will begin right now." He narrowed his eyes. "Mother, turn on the machine."

Karen's vision blurred as an immense amount of anger, of hatred, warped and blackened her thoughts. The dark energy moving within her intensified. Made her stomach sick, her head dizzy.

"Don't do it." Karen kept her gaze trained on Martha as she moved away from Janice and toward the shock therapy machine. "I'm warning you."

The two nightstands and dresser shook as if a freight train was speeding past the house. The items on top of the furniture rattled and clanked together. The water pitcher and glass fell from the nightstand, splashing their contents to the concrete floor.

As if someone were blowing up a balloon beyond its full capacity, Karen's energy became alarmingly taut. It suffocated her with rage, with the need for revenge. Some of the other objects around the room also toppled to the floor. The girl's head pounded. Her body went numb. Breathing became difficult. All of Karen's dark thoughts and energy collided.

And burst.

The basement windows shattered, along with the overhead light, sending shards of glass through the air. The brain monitor fell from the table. Martha quickly caught it and set it on the floor, then rushed to the electrotherapy machine.

"Hit the switch," Dr. Ryker shouted as the doors on the cabinet across the room swung open, and books, medical equipment and vials of what looked like drugs crashed to the floor.

Karen quickly met Janice's terrified gaze. *"I'm here with you, Karen."* Tears streamed from her mother's eyes as her voice filled Karen's head. *"Calm down. Save your energy. Please, honey, we need each other to survive this."*

The furniture stopped moving. Any objects still floating in the air fell to the concrete.

"Good. Relax and—"

Pain shot through Karen's skull as Dr. Ryker sent electricity through her brain. Every bit of the girl's misery became Celeste's: the stiffening of her muscles, her twitching body and exploding nerve endings.

Celeste prayed the girl's ghost would rip her away from the torture and take her back to the present day. Instead, Celeste was forced to suffer right along with Karen and deal with her agony. The girl's thoughts were frenzied. An array of emotions filled her head and heart. Until one of those emotions consumed all the rest.

Rage.

The rage was so damned strong. Celeste didn't just feel it. She owned it. Hated Dr. Ryker, his mother…his son for bringing her here.

"That was incredible." Dr. Ryker said, his voice distant, tinny. He leaned onto Karen's jerking body. "I knew the girl had the power, I just had no idea the strength of it. Imagine if we could control it. God, think of the government grants."

"It truly was incredible, dear," Martha said with pride, as if her son had been the one to move objects with his mind. "Your experiment was a success."

"Absolutely." He lifted himself off Karen, whose body periodically twitched, and removed her mouth guard. "I'd like to try again tomorrow."

Janice bent forward and, because her wrists were bound in front of her, she was able to rip the tape from her mouth. "A success? You took an innocent girl with an outstanding gift and shit all over it."

Although impressed and proud of her mom, Celeste ached as much as Karen did. Sleep. She needed sleep.

"I did no such thing." Dr. Ryker lifted the cabinet that had fallen, while Martha used a broom to sweep up the glass. "I freed her. Here's what you don't realize... Her parents are terrified of her. Their minister was still convinced Karen was possessed when he suggested they bring her to me. Guess what? Mom and Dad don't want her back. Ever. They signed a contract stating that she is now under my care."

"That's horrible."

"People don't want to accept the unexplainable. They want to blame the Devil or demonic possession. But you and I both know the mind is powerful."

"What you're doing is unethical. And out of your control."

"Sounds like you're challenging me." Dr. Ryker smiled. "Let me ask you this...how would you like to have Karen's ability to move objects?"

"It's bad enough that I see dead people. I want nothing to do with being telekinetic."

"Why not?"

"Look around the room. Look in the mirror, or at your mother. Both of you have cuts on your faces from when the windows and lamp shattered. I don't know if Karen intended for any of that to happen, but what if she didn't? What if she can't learn to control her gift? What if every time she became stressed or angry, she also became destructive?" Janice let out a tired sigh. "I don't want to own that kind of power and be held responsible for the damage my mind and emotions might cause."

"Aiden will be home soon." Martha glanced at the clock, and set the broom aside. "Why don't I take Janice back to her room?" she suggested, and used scissors to cut the tape around Janice's ankles. "When I come back, I'll help you clean."

Dr. Ryker began removing the restraints around Karen's body. "There're shards of glass on the bedding and the girl's clothes. Take a fresh gown from the drawer. Janice can tend to Karen while we clean," he said, lifting Karen in his arms.

Thankfully the girl kept her eyes open as Dr. Ryker left the room. Celeste had not been conscious when Aiden and Martha had brought her to their house. Because what she was witnessing had happened over thirty years ago, she hoped the basement hadn't changed much. She wanted to get a feel for the layout should she have an opportunity to run.

The basement wasn't exactly finished, but walls had been erected and doors had been hung. From her vantage point, she counted two doors before they reached another room. This one had no windows and, like her room, the cinder block had been painted white. A single bulb hung from the center of the room. There was a cot against the wall. The only other furniture was a plastic lawn chair and small table, a pitcher and glass on top of it.

Dr. Ryker placed Karen's limp body on the cot. As if weighted by cement, the girl's limbs felt too heavy to lift. Her mind was sluggish, her thoughts unclear. Having now experienced shock therapy herself, Celeste understood the immediate side effects, but also wondered if the telekinetic episode had anything to do with Karen's lack of energy.

After the doctor left the room, Martha set the hospital gown on the cot, then tore the tape from Janice's wrists. "Seth will be back for the girl shortly."

"Why are you helping him?" Janice asked.

"He's my son. He pays the mortgage, bills, groceries… I have no money of my own, so I have no choice."

"There's always a choice. What he's doing is unethical and inhumane."

Martha's face crumpled with worry and indecision. "You don't understand. Seth said that if I don't help him, he'd force me to leave. Who would care for my grandson? Last year, his mother left without a word. Seth is too busy with his work to pay attention to Aiden. The little boy needs me."

"But do you really want your grandson living in this environment? You can go to the police."

"The police? You want me to send my only child to prison? Deny my grandson a relationship with his father?"

"What if one of Seth's *patients* gets loose and hurts Aiden? What if the next time Karen lets loose her power the boy is accidentally injured or worse? This is wrong," Janice insisted. "Please help us. Make an anonymous call if you need to, but please just call the authorities. Please. Before something terrible happens that can't be undone."

Martha's eyes were filled with sadness as she glanced to Karen. "I have to go," she said.

"Even if you don't care about me or Karen, at least consider your grandson."

Martha gave her a curt nod. "I'll think about it," she said, then left the room, closing and locking the door.

Janice hurried to the cot. She knelt and brushed Karen's hair aside. "Oh, honey," she whispered, then draped her body over the girl and wept.

It had been over six years since Celeste had been held by her mother. Six years of grieving, of wishing things could have been different. Hearing her mother's voice now, and feeling her warmth, brought back so many memories…late night talks, long walks, baking and gardening together, helping at the family diner, snuggling on the couch and watching a movie. Since her mother's death, Celeste had longed to have one more cup of coffee with her mom. Just one. She wanted to tell Janice about John, Olivia and Mason. Tell her mom how much she'd meant to her, how much she loved her and the impact she'd made on her life. How she thought about her every single day, and still missed her terribly. Because the day her mom had died, a part of Celeste had died, too.

Except this moment wasn't real. Her mom and Karen no longer existed in the present day, but in the past where time didn't move forward. Even if she could communicate with her mother, this wasn't the Janice Risinski she'd known. Celeste didn't have a relationship with this Janice, didn't love her, didn't know anything about her. They didn't share a history. Not yet. But even if she never reconnected with her mom in the spirit world, she was grateful for this brief moment with her. To witness her strength and compassion. And to discover her mom had possessed the gift of telepathy.

Janice gently lifted Karen, then began changing the girl's clothes. Karen didn't speak, didn't think. Her mind had become a black void. Which terrified Celeste and had her wondering how many times the girl had been subjected to shock therapy.

"Karen, you need to stay strong and stay with me," Janice said as she settled the girl back onto the cot. She stroked her cheek. "Honey, can you hear me?"

Instead of responding, Karen closed her eyes, plunging Celeste into darkness. A simple phrase ran through the teen's sluggish mind... *Want to die.*

Celeste had thought the same in the wake of her shock therapy. After seeing her mom, she didn't want to die. She wanted to fight. These people needed to be stopped. Martha needed to pay for her crimes. The old nurse had to be the reason Karen's spirit hadn't passed to the other side. Celeste had read the case file on Dr. Ryker. Except to state that Martha had lived with her son, the woman's name had not otherwise been mentioned. How was that possible? Clearly the woman had taken part in her son's experiments. She'd also taken pleasure in tormenting Karen. How was it that no one knew this?

"Because they died."

As Karen's voice whispered through Celeste's head, bright light needled her eyes. Her stomach sick, her throat tightening with the urge to vomit, Celeste dragged in a ragged breath. Now back in her own body, and no longer ready to curl up and die, she searched the room for Karen. She jerked when Martha's wrinkled face came into view instead.

The old woman smiled. "What was that you were doing?"

Celeste licked her dry lips. "You mean sleeping?"

Martha's gaze grew suspicious. "Your eyes have been open for a couple hours."

"I've been told I sometimes sleep that way. It freaks out my husband."

Martha sat on the edge of the bed. "And has your husband told you that your eye color changes? The blue was incredibly pale while you were asleep."

"He's mentioned it. Can I please have water?"

"Of course."

"I'm not going to leave here," Celeste said, as the woman poured water from the pitcher into a plastic cup.

"Is that a question, or are you predicting your own future?"

"Why weren't you arrested with your son?" Celeste asked instead.

Martha brought the straw to Celeste's lips. "Who was alive to tell on me?"

"My mother."

"Ah, but your mother believed I was a victim of mental and verbal abuse. When I was brought in for questioning, I explained that I was just as much of a victim as my son's patients. Seth worried Aiden would be forced into foster care if I was also arrested, so he never said a word about my involvement."

That confirmed Celeste's suspicions. "Did you call the FBI on your son?"

The hint of a smile crossed the old woman's lips. "Now why would I do that?"

"Why would you encourage your grandson to get involved with something you know won't end well?" Celeste countered.

Martha set the cup on the nightstand, then reached behind her neck. "Very few things impress or surprise me. And I've seen a lot of things in my eighty-five years. When you repeated, almost verbatim, the conversation Aiden and I had with my son at the prison, I admit to getting goose bumps." She finished removing her gold necklace, and held it up for Celeste to see. Dangling from the chain was a small red ladybug pendant about the size of a dime. "Seth gave this to me on Mother's Day in 1960." She studied the ladybug. "He was twelve at the time." Martha placed the necklace into Celeste's palm.

"Why are you giving this to me?"

Martha leaned closer. "Before I die, I want one person to know the truth. And, I admit, I've been wanting to brag about what I've done and seen. If you're as good a psychic as I think you are, then you will be the first to know everything about me."

Celeste closed her hand around the necklace and shook her head. "Confess to a priest. I don't want to know. I just want to leave."

"But that's not going to happen, which makes you the perfect person to know all my secrets."

"You're not worried I'll tell Aiden?"

Martha grinned. "That boy loves his grandma too much to believe anything negative you might tell him about me."

The door opened and Aiden stepped inside. "Grandma, we need to change our plans."

Martha looked over her shoulder. "Why? What's wrong?"

"It's George. He's going downhill fast, so I think we should work on him this evening and deal with her tomorrow after church."

Martha sighed. "I'll be right there."

"Okay, I'll get him ready," he said, then left.

"What are you going to do to George?" Celeste asked, wondering if he too was psychic, or had special gifts like Karen.

Martha walked to the door. "We're going to perform brain surgery."

Celeste's stomach dropped. "That's insane."

"Be glad we're doing it. Aiden finished medical school, and as an intern he assisted with many surgeries, but he's never performed one on his own. Better he practice on a dying man than you." She started to turn, then stopped. "If you want to see insanity, look into my past."

"Again, why? And don't tell me it's because you want me to know something about you. Or because you want to brag about the past."

"But that's the truth." Martha cocked her white head. "Maybe," she said, then left the room, closing the door behind her.

"It has to be a trick." Karen appeared next to Celeste. *"Don't trust her."*

"What do you know about Martha?"

"Ssh. Talk with your mind, not your mouth. You don't want them to hear you." The ghost's yellow aura darkened to burnt orange. *"I know what she did to me. I'm not sure about the others. They won't talk to me."*

Dr. Ryker killed five people, you're one of them. Where are they? Maybe they can help us, Celeste said, recalling what she remembered from the Ryker case file.

"Remember when you were in my body and Dr. Ryker carried you to your mother's room? Next to where she was kept is another room. It's Oscar's. The door is always closed and I can't get inside. I hear him and I try to talk to him, but he tells me to go away. Holly and Thomas are in the other rooms. They won't talk to me, either." Karen's aura returned to yellow. *"There's an old coal room on the other side of the basement by the furnace and hot water tank. Sometimes I hear a woman crying in there. Every time I've tried to talk to her, she stops but says nothing."* She frowned. *"There was another woman. I saw her once during an experiment. I remember one time Aiden came into my room. He was just a little boy then. He said something about the woman in the attic. I think her name was Darla."*

Darla, the woman who could predict the future. Celeste had read that when the FBI had raided the Ryker home, they'd found Darla Kemper's decomposing body in the attic. Her head had been shaved and stitched. Later, after an autopsy, the pathologist had determined Darla had had part of her brain removed. She'd died from an aneurysm, likely due to the surgery.

Celeste also remembered reading about Oscar Martinez, who, according to Dr. Ryker, supposedly possessed the ability to soak in electrical energy, then redirect it. Oscar had, unfortunately, died from electrocution. Dr. Ryker had given the man electroshock therapy to see if he would absorb the energy. Oscar had absorbed the voltage, but it had fried his brain and internal organs. The medical examiner had noted that there was even charring on his heart, brain, lungs and kidneys. There were also two others, Holly Simon and Thomas Hill. Holly died from a heart attack, possibly brought on by too much electroconvulsive therapy, and Thomas had, like Karen, a lobotomy that had gone wrong.

The woman in the coal room was new to her. If there'd been a body there, the FBI would've discovered it.

I know about Oscar and Darla—the woman in the attic—along with Holly and Thomas. But the FBI only found five bodies. Are you sure you've heard a woman crying from the coal room?

Karen's aura turned burnt orange again. "Why would I lie to you? Since my death, if the door to this room is open, I can leave. But I can't leave the basement. Once Dr. Ryker was arrested and the experiments stopped, I roamed the rooms looking for a way out of here." Worry lined her face. "Do you think God forgot about me? Or was my gift from the Devil and this is my punishment?"

You said I was telepathic, Celeste began. *And I've never had a telepathic experience until today. I'm not even sure I can qualify our communication as telepathy since you're a ghost. But when I was in your body I experienced my mom's telepathic ability, so maybe I am. Either way, I don't believe our gifts are the work of something evil. I've been to the light. It's a beautiful place and you deserve to be there.*

"But how do I get there?" Her aura paled. "I need to leave this place. I'm so lonely. Until you came, there was no warmth. Only cold darkness. The last time I felt any warmth or compassion was with Janice, and that moment was so brief, sometimes I think I imagined it."

Celeste's eyes filled with tears. *I want to help you. I think the only way to do that is to make sure Martha is punished. Unless Aiden did something to you.*

"No. He was just a boy. He thought I was cool and called me Jean Grey from X-Men."

Aiden was no longer a cool kid. Because of his misguided and delusional admiration of his father, he was becoming just like him. A monster.

I have Martha's necklace. I can do a reading and learn more about the woman. Maybe I'll find a way to get to her.

"Don't waste your time on a reading. Work on getting out of here."

Celeste hid her irritation. *How? Unless you can remove my restraints, I'm stuck here. They won't even let me get out of bed to use the bathroom.* Instead, they'd humiliated her by forcing her to use a bed pan.

"Use your gift. I know telepathy is new to you, but it's a gift you've always had."

How do you know?

The girl shrugged. "I sensed it. Like minds and all that."

Like minds and all that didn't work for her. But maybe there was some truth to what Karen had *sensed*. Karen had never met Janice until Dr. Ryker had brought her into the room for an experiment, and yet the two had easily made mental exchanges. Was it possible that Janice had had this skill all along and hadn't known it? After all, she'd never attempted to reach out to another person using only her mind. Why would she?

"It's about focus," Karen continued. "Planting images or thoughts into peoples' minds. You have a husband and children. Why not try reaching out to one of them?"

Celeste pictured John and her babies. She imagined how distraught and angry he was at the moment, and worried how he was handling the situation while playing the role of both mom and dad. Though she believed he could be receptive to mental communication, his mind might be too plagued with fear and anxiety for him to pick up on the message she would send him.

There was Maxine, Ian, Eden...*Olivia*. Yes, Olivia. The adults would be dealing with grownup worries and emotions. While Olivia was old enough to probably understand that something was wrong, and Mommy wasn't there, her three-year-old mind wouldn't be as muddled as that of an adult's.

My daughter is like me. She can see and speak to the dead. I think she would be receptive, but she's so young. I'm worried I won't be able to get my message across to her.

Karen's aura became blindingly bright as she smiled. *"Try. Tell her who has you. Tell her you love her."*

While Celeste still wasn't convinced she had the gift of telepathy, she had to do something before Martha and Aiden experimented on her brain. *Okay, I'll try. But I think I'll still try to reach my husband first.*

The ghost beamed. *"Focus on him, on his image, then on what you want him to see or hear. Focus, Celeste. Focus…"*

Celeste closed her eyes. Saw John lying on the hotel bed, looking adorably sweet and sexy holding their sleeping children. And she focused…

CHAPTER 6

John and Celeste's house, Chicago, Illinois
Saturday, 5:12 p.m. Central Daylight Time

PEANUT BUTTER AND jelly sandwiches were on the menu this evening. Since they were supposed to be on vacation, there wasn't any food in the house, and John hadn't had the foresight to pull something out of the freezer. He wasn't hungry, but Liv needed to eat. Mason, who had an entire shelf in the pantry dedicated to his baby food, was set. Except, he'd been unusually lethargic all day, and hadn't wanted anything to do with his lunch or afternoon bottle.

The doorbell rang. When he didn't hear Ruth, their black lab, bark, John wondered if he should have picked her up from Ian's—who was dog sitting for them—on their way back from Maxine's. Ruth was part of the family, and would provide a sense of normalcy for the kids.

As he made his way from the kitchen, he decided to ask both Ian and Maxine their opinion about the dog. Then again, he had bigger questions to ask the two of them as well. At three, there was no way Olivia knew Celeste's mother's name. Yet Olivia had claimed Janice was Ian and Maxine's secret. Which made little sense to him. Ian and Maxine had met socially. But Maxine hadn't known Janice. As for Ian, other than Celeste turning out to be Janice and his love child, he couldn't come up with another reason for there to be a secret regarding Celeste's mother.

When John opened the front door, Ian's fiancée, Cami Carlyle, fell into his arms.

"Oh, John," she said, holding him tightly. "I'm so sorry."

John hugged her and looked behind her at his father-in-law, who stood on the porch holding a casserole dish and a brown grocery bag. "Thanks for coming, but what's all this?" he asked, breaking away from Cami's bear hug.

"Dinner," Ian said, handing over the grocery bag.

Once inside, the melancholy mood of the house shifted. Grammy Cami had a way of brightening a room, and although Olivia and Mason weren't blood relations, Cami's love for the kids was obvious. In a few minutes, she had Olivia and Mason smiling, and his house smelling wonderful.

John still had no interest in food. All he could think about was Celeste and the people who'd abducted her. Still, he tried to put on a happy face for the kids. He sat through dinner, and noticed that no one, except Mason, ate much. When they were through, and Olivia declined a cupcake for dessert, John's concerns intensified. His daughter *never* turned down a chocolate cupcake.

"Why don't you and Ian talk while I give the kids a bath?" Cami suggested as she helped clean up the dishes.

John hadn't heard from FBI agent, Laura Grabowski, since before the reading he'd done with Olivia. He also hadn't gotten a call from anyone at CORE regarding the leads he'd given Ian. Even if Ian hadn't any new information, he'd like a moment alone with the man. John had a question that needed answering.

"If you don't mind, that'd be great," John said.

Olivia tugged at the hem of Cami's shirt. "Bubbles?"

"Of course. Grammy Cami wasn't sure if you had any, so I brought my own. And guess what? My bubbles smell like strawberries."

When Olivia giggled, and Cami had Mason laughing after she gave him a tickle and a silly face, John relaxed. Slightly. Momentarily. If he didn't get Celeste back with them, this would forever be their world. No mommy, just him and occasional visits from relatives. That couldn't happen. This couldn't be their new reality. He and Celeste had plans. Had their future mapped. They were supposed to grow old together. Eventually move south during the winter months and enjoy the beach and sunny skies once they'd retired.

Damn it. He shoved a hand through his hair and tried to control his emotions. He did not want to live without Celeste. She was his world. His light when it was dark.

"How about a beer?" Ian asked, reaching into the refrigerator.

"Sure," John said, not really wanting anything, but hoping a couple beers on an empty stomach would help him fall asleep tonight.

Once Cami had the kids upstairs, John led Ian into the living room. "How's Ruth?" John asked.

"She's a good dog. We'll keep her for as long as you need." Ian grinned. "Except now that we've had a dog in the house, Cami has decided she has her heart set on getting one."

"You've been dog sitting for less than a day."

"It doesn't take Cami long to know what she wants." Ian set his beer on the coffee table. "I heard from Agent Grabowski."

Why would she contact Ian and not him? John took a long drink to keep from snapping.

"FBI agents checked into George Meadows' background," Ian continued. "With permission from his family, they searched his house, talked with North Bethesda PD...they've got nothing. The man didn't drink, didn't smoke or use drugs."

"What about religion?" John asked, thinking about how the old woman was involved in her church.

"According to his family and friends, George was agnostic."

John pushed a hand through his hair. "There has to be some connection."

"Logically, that makes sense. Except you and I both know that logic doesn't always come into play with criminals." Ian reached for his beer. "It could be Meadows was a random choice."

John shook his head. "I don't believe that. They *targeted* Celeste. They came from the east, got what they wanted, then headed back home. Whether it's something related to my past or yours, they wanted her. So don't even try to tell me Celeste was a random choice, too."

"Their travel itinerary gives me every reason to believe they came for Celeste, but I can't say the same for George Meadows."

John understood where Ian was coming from. Under other circumstances—ones that didn't involve his wife—he would agree. But he wanted Meadows to be a target, too. He wanted a link. He wanted a connection that would lead them to his wife.

"Is Meadows a dead end then?" John asked.

"To the FBI? For now. But I have Rachel looking deeper. She might spot something the FBI haven't. Meanwhile, she's looked into churches with First Baptist in the name, and found there are twenty-seven in Maryland. There are also another eighteen Baptist churches in the state without *first* in the name. Rachel checked Maryland death records from last year, too, hoping to find Mrs. Smith. Fifty-three deceased women had that last name. Assuming Mrs. Smith was elderly, she was able to narrow the list down to thirty-nine."

"If this Mrs. Smith is deceased."

"Right." Ian nodded. "If she's not, Rachel found there are thirty-two nursing homes in Maryland. The problem I have with all of this is we're not sure if these people are living in Maryland. If we check with each church and look into the Smith lead, but come up empty, we'll have to find another route, or search additional states along the east coast."

"We don't have that kind of time." John rubbed his temple and tried to pull his thoughts together, come up with a plan of action. Sitting around and doing nothing led to dwelling on possibilities and outcomes he didn't want to consider. "Tomorrow morning Olivia will do another reading. Hopefully we'll be able to get to that stack of mail I saw on the kidnappers' table. If not, and if the kids can stay with Cami or Eden, I'll fly to Maryland and start hitting churches."

"Rachel has already reached out to the churches that were open. She's waiting to hear back from them regarding a parishioner named Phyllis. She plans to contact the other churches in the morning."

"What about the photo we have of the old woman? Did she send it over?"

"Yes. No one from the parish offices recognized her, but everyone Rachel spoke to was cooperative and willing to help. They'd said they would show the picture to church members during Sunday services." Ian looked toward the stairs when Cami and Olivia's singing floated from the bathroom. He frowned. "I missed so many years of Celeste's life. I'm grateful I can capture glimpses of what I missed through Olivia." He looked away and cleared his throat. "Do you know Celeste still doesn't call me Dad?"

John wasn't in the mood for an emotional heart-to-heart with his father-in-law. While he appreciated that Ian was doing what he could to find Celeste, and that Cami was helping with the kids, he wanted them to leave. Once Mason was in his crib, he planned to attempt a reading with Olivia. Too many things could happen to Celeste during the night, and he didn't want to wait until the morning to try to connect with her or the kidnappers.

"Sure she does," John said, because he wasn't a jerk and he understood Ian was worried, too. "I've heard her introduce you as her father many times."

"But she doesn't *call* me Dad." Ian half shrugged. "I guess once in a while she'll say it, but mostly I'm just Ian. The sperm donor who wasn't there for her. I'm much more than that. The moment I found out she existed, I was in love. She was my girl, my baby. And I couldn't hold her or do anything for her but watch from a distance."

"Because of Janice," John said, holding his gaze.

"I hold no resentment toward her."

"You say that now."

"Meaning?"

"She's dead. Let's face it. You screwed up. You had the girl, got her pregnant, then chose your work over her," John said, bringing up Janice's kidnapping. He wanted to know why Olivia would think Celeste's mother was connected to both Ian and Maxine.

Ian's face reddened. "I knew every member on the team assembled to rescue her. She was in good hands."

"And you lost her to one of the team members who ended up raising your love child. Meanwhile, Janice never bothered to tell Celeste about you, or let you be involved in your daughter's life. Why?"

Ian pulled in a slow breath and set his beer back on the table. "I know you're hurting, so am I, but you're being an asshole. When it comes to Celeste, I've made mistakes. You know that. I've been open and honest with you about Celeste and Janice." He leaned forward. "Every person who works for me thinks I'm a manipulative son of a bitch. So the hell what? I am. I make no apologies when it comes to my business. But when it comes to family, I'm no bullshit. If I could make it so I was in Celeste's position, and she was here, I would. I'd give my life for my daughter."

John ignored the stab of guilt piercing his chest, because Ian was lying. "Open and honest?" he repeated. "Then explain to me why my daughter thinks you and Maxine have a secret that involves Janice."

"Olivia told you this?" Ian asked, then drained his beer.

"She specifically said Janice. How would she know her name?"

"She's a bright little girl. I'm sure she's heard Celeste say Janice's name."

John shook her head. "Whenever Celeste has shown Liv a picture of Janice, she's always referred to her mom as Grandma in heaven, or Mommy's mommy. To double check, I showed Olivia a picture of Janice and asked her to tell me her name, and she gave me Grandma in heaven, not Janice." He leaned forward and rested his forearms on his knees. "I think Olivia's gift is evolving. I don't know if it's because she's getting a little older and becoming more aware, but there's been a change in her. A powerful one. She knows something she can't explain, so you explain it for her.

What's the secret?"

Ian stood. "I need another beer or something stronger."

"Vigo drank all my booze and I haven't replaced it yet."

Ian stared at him for a moment, then went into the kitchen. He returned with two fresh beers and set them on the coffee table. Instead of sitting, he walked to one of the built-in bookshelves flanking the fireplace, and picked up a frame holding a picture of Celeste and Janice. "From the moment you met my daughter, life has been…interesting, hasn't it?"

"That's an understatement," he said, just as Olivia let out a high-pitched scream.

"John," Cami called, panicked. "Come quick!"

John rushed up the stairs and came to an abrupt halt. Olivia stood in the hallway, her face pale, her eyes wide and welling with tears. She stared ahead, but not at him. He glanced to Cami, who held Mason. "What happened?" he asked, going to his daughter and kneeling in front of her.

"I don't know. Everything was fine. She was laughing and singing just minutes ago. We were about to head downstairs for milk and a snack when she stopped and started screaming."

Regret settled on his shoulders. His little girl had gone through a lot in less than twenty-four hours, and he worried he'd pushed her too hard today. "Liv? Honey, what's wrong?" He rubbed her stiff arms.

Terror crossed her face, but she didn't answer.

Concerned, he gave her a slight shake. "Olivia," he said, louder and with a stern tone.

She blinked and met his gaze. A tear slipped down her cheek. "Daddy?"

Oh, hell. Had his daughter gone into a trance? Whenever Celeste had fallen into one, she'd often had the same faraway look, too. "What's the matter, honey?"

More tears fell. "I scared."

"Of what?"

"White an yellow girl."

White and yellow girl? "There's no girl here like that."

Olivia pointed to her head. "She here."

"Like in a dream?" he asked, hoping that was the case and Olivia wasn't seeing ghosts in their house.

She shrugged. "Her scare me," she said, then burst into tears. "She haf Mommy."

Unsure what to make of whatever Olivia thought she saw, and worried about his daughter's mental state, he pulled her to him and lifted her into his arms. "Ssh." He ran a hand over her damp curls. "The girl isn't real and can't hurt you."

Olivia leaned back and cupped John's cheeks. "Mommy say like her."

"You think Mommy wants you to like the white and yellow girl?"

She bobbed her head, and pushed her lip out in a pout. "Livy don't," she said, and continued to cry.

"These two have had a long day." Cami cuddled Mason against her chest. "I think it's night-night time."

After Ian and Cami had helped put the kids to bed, John joined them in the living room. "I'm worried about Olivia," he said. "The reading, what she saw at the hotel…I think it's too much for her to understand."

Cami hugged herself. "I'm worried about her, too. Maybe you should reconsider going to Maxine's tomorrow."

"If Rachel or the FBI comes up with a solid lead, we might not need to do another reading," Ian said.

"And if they don't?" John blew out a breath. "Let's see how Liv is in the morning," he suggested, torn between forcing his daughter to see things she shouldn't and the need to find his wife. "Either way, plan to meet at Maxine's at eight." As Ian and Cami headed out the door, John stopped his father-in-law. "And also plan on finishing our earlier conversation."

Irritation momentarily flashed in Ian's eyes. With a curt nod, he and Cami left.

Exhausted, John shut down the house, then went up to his

room. When he walked in, he found Olivia on his bed and buried under the covers. "What are you doing in here?" he asked, snuggling next to her.

"Liv scared. I stay wif Daddy."

"You can stay with me. I'll always protect you."

As he kissed her forehead, then turned out the lights, he worried if he would be able to keep that promise. Regardless of what he'd told Ian and Cami, unless a miracle happened overnight, he *would* use Olivia tomorrow. He needed to know Celeste was okay. Damn it, he needed her home.

The Ryker Residence, Silver Spring, Maryland
Saturday, 6:32 p.m. Eastern Daylight Time

HOW DO YOU *know if a person has received your message?* Celeste asked the ghost hovering above her.

"Unless they tell you, or respond back, I'm not sure."

But when I was in your body, I heard Martha and Dr. Ryker's thoughts. I also heard the thoughts of a boy you pictured. You do know you were never a freak, right?

Karen's aura dimmed. "*I never thought I was, and I never believed my parents thought that, either. Not until Dr. Ryker told me they didn't want me."*

That's not true. I read about what happened here and at Dr. Ryker's sentencing. Your parents addressed the court and made it clear they had no idea he was using you for experiments. They said they had called and tried to see you multiple times, but Dr. Ryker told them you were making progress and he didn't want that to be disrupted. The day before the FBI came here, your mom and dad claimed they'd talked with Dr. Ryker again, and said they had threatened to call the police if they couldn't see you. Celeste considered the conversation between Martha and Janice. *I'm wondering if Martha was the one who called the FBI.*

"The day before?" Karen's aura darkened, became muddy. *"I was already dead."*

Tears stung Celeste's eyes. *I know. And I'm so sorry for how much you suffered. This should have never happened.*

The ghost nodded. *"I've often wondered what my life would have been like if I'd lived. If I would've married and had kids."* Her forehead creased. *"I don't think I was meant to live a long life. My gift became more powerful as I got older. As you saw, I didn't know how to control it. Maybe there's a reason I was put in Dr. Ryker's path."*

I don't know that I believe that.

"I'm still here, which makes me think it's true. Something hasn't been fixed."

You mean Martha is still free.

"Maybe," Karen said, her voice filled with sadness. *"What did you show your daughter?"*

The same thing I tried to show John and Maxine...you. I also kept thinking about Ryker, hoping one of them would remember the case. As Celeste stared at the young albino ghost, at her pale eyes, face and hair, she realized she hoped Olivia hadn't received her message. Karen didn't scare her, but Celeste wasn't three years old. *Even if Olivia heard me, she might not be able to repeat the name or describe you to John.*

"It's difficult to know from a distance." For the first time since Celeste had seen her, Karen smiled. *"I used to put ideas and images in my little brother's head. I would suggest he clean my room or do the dishes for me."* Her smile fell. *"The Christmas before I came here, I planted the image of a stereo I really wanted in my parents' minds. It was the first time I'd done anything like that to them."*

Did you get it?

Karen shook her head. *"No. My parents got upset and scared. When they confronted me about it, I lost control and accidentally broke things...with my mind. That's when they took me to our minister, and how I ended up here."*

You said that was the first time you planted an image in their minds, but did you ever read their thoughts?

"Never on purpose. They came to me when I was feeling sick or sad. If my energy was low or dark, my gift became stronger. Maybe

that's why Martha and Dr. Ryker's thoughts were so clear to me."

What about telekinesis? Celeste asked. *Was that also stronger when you were down?*

"No. I've been able to move things since I was about seven. I never told anyone, though, because even then I knew it wasn't normal. Since I didn't look like everyone else, I figured I should keep it to myself." Karen studied her for a moment. "What's it like to see the past and talk to ghosts?"

It can be scary. There've been times when I've wished my gift away. But it's who I am, and I believe there's a reason I was blessed with being psychic.

"To help people like me?"

I think so.

"But you won't be able to help me if you die. Martha will go unpunished."

I still don't understand why she wants me to see her past. Celeste tightened her fist. The old woman's necklace warmed her palm and made it clammy. *I don't want to know what she's done.*

"You should do it now. Like you said, you might discover something about her that will help set us free."

Willing to try anything at this point, Celeste closed her eyes. While she preferred to use a pen and paper to take her where she needed to go, that wasn't an option. Since she'd been able to perform a reading for Aiden without pen and paper, she was confident she could do the same with Martha's necklace.

Drawing in a steadying breath, she concentrated on the necklace. Saw the thin gold chain. In her mind, it twisted and looped. Grew longer, then coiled like a snake. It unwound and spiraled again, creating the vortex she needed to move through time. Placing all of her energy onto the bright light at the center, she moved through a pivoting tunnel, the walls around her revealing quick, blurry images of people she didn't recognize. As she neared the vortex, a force propelled her forward into a blindingly bright light. The tunnel walls fell away. She blinked several times and checked her surroundings.

The room was filled with at least two dozen young women, all wearing baggy, thin, short-sleeved dresses. None of them wore shoes or socks, and each of them had similar short bobbed haircuts. Some of the women sat on wooden benches, while others either sat or lay on the floor. The lighting was poor. The windows were covered in a thick film and chain link guards. A few women moaned and grunted. Others talked to themselves. Some slept. One woman who was seated on the floor, her legs bent at the knees exposing her lack of underwear, continuously banged the back of her head against the brick wall that had been painted a putrid green.

When the door opened, Celeste glanced to the corner of the room. A woman who appeared to be in her thirties and dressed in a vintage nurse's uniform, white cap and all, stepped inside with a large man, also dressed in white. The nurse adjusted her ebony cat-eye glasses and looked around the room, her gaze stopping on the woman banging her head against the wall. She and the man approached. As they neared, Celeste recognized a young Martha Ryker, and now wished she hadn't come to this place in time. With the way the patients looked and acted, this couldn't be a regular hospital.

"Take that one," Martha said, pointing at the woman against the wall.

The man picked her up as if she weighed nothing, which Celeste guessed to be true. All of the inmates here were thin and boney. The woman didn't protest. Instead she curled against the large man's chest and stuck her thumb into her mouth as if she were a child, and let him carry her from the room.

Celeste caught up with them in the hallway, watched as Martha locked the door behind her, then she followed the trio through several corridors and down two flights of steps. When they reached the lower level, Martha opened a door. "Put her inside," she said. After the man had done as he was told, she slipped him money, then he disappeared back up the stairs.

Martha quickly walked to another door and opened it. Sunlight spilled into the darkened hallway, along with the silhouette of a person. "Hurry, my shift ends in an hour," she said.

A man, dressed in street clothes from the '60s, entered the building, and followed Martha to the room where the woman had been left. He gave Martha money. "How much time do I have?"

"No more than thirty minutes. And make sure you don't leave any marks on her, understand. You bruised the last girl."

The man frowned. "I did?"

"Yes. One of our staff saw the bruises when he was taking her to the morgue. We can't have that, otherwise I won't let you in here anymore."

"Sorry. I must've gotten carried away," the man said. "I'll be extra careful."

Martha clutched the money. "You do that," she said. Once he was in the room and the door was closed behind him, Martha lifted the hem of her dress, then slipped the money into the top of her stockings.

Curious, Celeste walked through the wood door. Regret slammed into her the moment she did, and she immediately went back into the hallway. While she hadn't expected to step into the middle of an art class, she hadn't been prepared to witness the woman's rape, either.

"You horrible bitch," Celeste said, even though she knew Martha couldn't hear her. "How could you be so depraved and cruel?"

Celeste followed Martha down the hallway. When she saw a sign stating, *Property of Forest Haven*, she paused. Shit. Not too long ago she'd watched a documentary on abandoned asylums. Forest Haven was one of them, and had been closed in the early '90s. For years, its patients had allegedly suffered physical, mental and sexual abuse. Hundreds of people had died there due to neglect and medical incompetence, and the staff had buried the dead in a mass grave.

And Martha had worked there. A place filled with the forgotten and unwanted, the perfect place for a vile woman who had no compassion and clearly no conscience.

As Celeste caught up with Martha, she was pushed forward and thrown into another room. Martha was there, along with the poor woman she'd prostituted. The woman was on the floor, her body motionless, her eyes open but unseeing, as if she were in a catatonic state. Martha bent down, pinched the woman's nose and pressed her hand under her chin. As the minutes passed, the woman's body stiffened. She blinked several times, then finally went slack.

Martha stood. "Larry," she called as she brushed her hands along her skirt.

The large hospital orderly from earlier entered the room.

"Don't record this death, and don't tell anyone about it. Just put her in the grave with the others."

Larry shook his head. "This is getting too risky. I want a bigger cut."

Martha smiled. "And I want to go to your house and slice open your wife and children." She stepped forward. "Do as you're told. Remember, if you tell on me, you'll only implicate yourself. Look around you. Prison is only a step up from this hellhole."

Celeste was shoved forward again. As if Martha's life had been turned into a long movie trailer, she watched the woman torture other Forest Haven patients, witnessed her give electroshock therapy without the assistance of a doctor or anyone else. Saw her injecting people with drugs, then laughing as they convulsed. Celeste was pushed into a small brick room unlike the ones at Forest Haven. A young woman with long dark hair and a healthy figure was there, holding up her hands.

"You don't have to do this. I'll leave. I swear," the woman promised.

Martha's shadowy figure came into view beneath the lone light bulb hanging from the ceiling. This Martha looked just like the one from the '80s. "Oh, but I do," she said, slamming a mallet against the woman's head.

The woman dropped to the ground. Martha bent, checked her

pulse, then hit her again. "Larry," she called, wiping blood from her face with a towel.

The door opened, and the orderly from Forest Haven, only years older, stepped into the room carrying a long canvas duffle bag. He looked to the dead woman on the floor, then back at Martha. "We're even after this. I don't owe you anything more."

Martha gave her hair a little fluff. "Hmm. I'm not so sure about that. Your secret is very juicy. How would your wife and grown children feel about your fetish for young boys?"

Scowling, Larry opened the duffle bag, then began stuffing the brunette inside it. "When will enough be enough?"

"Never."

Larry tossed the mallet inside the bag, then zipped it. "What the hell is wrong with you?" He stood and faced her. "Why do you murder and hurt people? At least my *secret* gives me pleasure."

"Because I can." She smiled. "And who said I don't get any pleasure out of what I do?" She shooed him with her hand. "Go. Put her with the others."

"What about her luggage?"

"Burn it in the hospital incinerator." Martha slipped money from her pants pocket, then handed it to Larry. "Because I'm nice, here's a bonus."

After Larry had pocketed the money, then opened the door, Celeste realized they were in the basement of the Ryker house. She immediately recognized the hallway and doors from when she'd been in Karen's body, and figured she must be standing in the old coal room. She glanced to the duffle bag, and now understood why Karen claimed to have heard crying coming from here. The woman's body might have been removed from the house, but not her spirit.

Martha Ryker's movie trailer suddenly began playing again, then slowed to a stop. Celeste was now in a kitchen covered with avocado and gold wallpaper. The stove, refrigerator and dishwasher were also gold, along with the linoleum floor and frilly curtains hanging above the sink.

Martha pulled a roast from the oven, then checked the temperature, just as a younger version of Dr. Ryker entered the room. "Smells good," he said.

"It'll be ready shortly." She placed the pan back into the oven. "Where's Aiden?"

"Playing in the backyard." Dr. Ryker sat at the kitchen table, tapping the heels of his shoes against the floor. "I need to talk to you about something."

Martha wiped her hand on a kitchen towel as she turned to face him. "Oh? Is everything okay?"

"No. Sally is gone."

Martha rolled her eyes. "Your wife is always out and about and spending your hard-earned money. When was the last time she bothered to cook a meal or clean the house?"

"I mean, she left." He rubbed his forehead and stood. "Her clothes are gone, so are all of her toiletries and our suitcases. I checked the office files. She took her birth certificate and social security card, but left her credit cards behind."

Martha's dark brows pulled together in a V. "Did she leave a note?"

"Not that I can find." He pushed both hands through his hair. "I checked the safe. Two grand is missing."

Martha gasped. "The bitch. Oh, Seth, I'm so sorry. I know you love Sally, but any woman who would abandon her husband and son is a horrible creature."

Celeste remembered how Aiden had said his mother had left when he was around nine years old, and that he hadn't heard from her since. Now she wondered if the woman in the duffle bag was Sally Ryker.

"It doesn't make sense," Dr. Ryker said. "She never once showed any indication that she was unhappy."

"Well, you're the psychiatrist. You would know."

"Of course I would. Yes, I don't think she liked the long hours I've been putting in with the FBI, but she certainly didn't complain about the extra income." He hung his head. "How am I going to explain this to Aiden? Poor kid. He's barely nine. He's not going to understand any of this. *I* don't even understand."

"Maybe she left because of him, not you," Martha suggested.

"He's a good kid."

"A brilliant child…who has Asperger's syndrome, which would actually require her to work a little harder at being a good mom."

"But she was a good mom." He stood. "Maybe she met someone else."

"That's very possible. I've seen her eyeing young men at the grocery store." Martha walked over to her son and took his hands in hers. "I'm sorry. I shouldn't say anything more about Sally. I never cared much for her, but I know you loved her."

"I truly did."

"You can't let Sally's abandonment hurt your focus. Aiden will need you now more than ever. And your work is so important."

"That's not what the government thinks."

Martha cocked her head. "But I thought you got along well with those FBI people."

"Not them. I heard back from both the Air Force and Army. They won't give me any funding, nor will they entertain my theories about psychics. They said my ideas are ridiculous and something from a science fiction movie. Which is a load of garbage. It's not public record, but I talked with a guy who used to be part of a super-spy program run by both military divisions. From what he told me, they're not creating super-spies, they're creating super-failures."

"You don't need the government to run your experiments. Our basement is large. We can buy medical equipment," Martha smiled. "And I am, after all, a nurse. All you need are volunteering patients."

Dr. Ryker let go of his mother's hands. "I don't know…"

Celeste was moved through time again. She cringed and covered her mouth when she saw Karen's pale body on a table, the top of her scalp pulled back, a portion of her skull gone and her brain exposed. As bile rose in her throat, Celeste was ripped from the room and placed on a sidewalk outside of a Laundromat.

Wearing dark sunglasses, Martha, still with salt and pepper hair, stood in front of a payphone. She lifted the receiver, put a coin in the slot, then dialed 911. "You need to go to Dr. Seth Ryker's house on Quail Hollow in Silver Spring," she said, adjusting her voice so that it was nothing like her natural tone. "There's been a murder."

The street and Laundromat faded, only to be replaced with the Ryker kitchen, which had been updated with white appliances and the wallpaper had been removed. Martha, her hair now snow-white, sat at the table with Aiden, who held a letter. Celeste moved closer and read over Aiden's shoulder.

> *I know all about Janice and what you did to her. Guess what? She has a daughter, and she's even stronger than her mother. If you're still experimenting on psychics, here's her address.*
>
> *~ V*
>
> *P.S. Celeste is Ian Scott's daughter.*

"You're a brilliant man, dear," Martha said as she lifted her coffee mug. "Don't worry about your father. He'll come around once you've put his theories to the test and succeeded."

"But what if I don't succeed? What if the woman dies? We would go to prison."

"Then we get rid of the evidence."

Aiden chuckled. "You watch too much TV. This is real life. It's not that easy to get rid of a body."

A small smile played along Martha's mouth. "Well, you are the genius doctor, so you're probably right. I'm just an old fool who wants to see my son free from prison before I die."

Aiden let out a sigh, and took his grandmother's hand. "You're not a fool, and if I'm such a genius, why couldn't I pass the boards? I took that test four times."

"But you did assist in dozens of surgeries as an intern, correct?"

He nodded. "Not brain surgery, though."

"You have your father's notes, and there's always the Internet."

Aiden smiled. "YouTube does have videos of people undergoing brain surgery."

"While awake? Because we won't be able to give her an anesthetic." When he nodded again, Martha added, "Excellent, but I think we should have a practice patient first. I have a gentleman in mind. His name is George Meadows. During the year your father was prepping our basement for his clinic, he was also looking for psychic volunteers. George contacted Seth. Your dad tested him and discovered he was, indeed, psychic. Not very powerful, but for the purposes of his experiments, George would've made a good subject. But George had to back out due to a death in his family. Which was why Seth chose to bring Janice into the program."

"It's all her fault Dad got arrested."

"It no longer matters. Anyway, we can also use George's credit card and license plate when we travel to Chicago to get the girl."

"And you think I'm the genius," Aiden said with a smile.

"I'm street-smart, you're book-smart. Together we're unstoppable." She leaned forward. "Together we're going to get your dad out of prison."

Celeste was thankfully pulled from the room and forced back into the Ryker basement. And not in the room where they'd been keeping her. This had been where her mother had stayed. Except it contained more than a cot and plastic patio furniture. Instead, there was a high-powered lamp aimed at a cot holding a man. He lay prone, with his face resting inside a foamy round massage pillow and his limbs hanging over the edge of the cot. A metal cart with scalpels, varying sizes of forceps, and other medical tools was also next to the bed. Near the man's shoulders, Aiden and Martha each sat on a stool. On a table next to Aiden was an opened laptop and book. Celeste moved closer, then quickly looked away.

Oh, my God.

Celeste gagged on bile again. Her skin crawled as she viewed a portion of the man's brain. Although tempted to leave this place, she wasn't ready to be back in her restraints. Plus, if she survived this ordeal, she wanted to be able to tell the authorities everything she could about Martha and Aiden. And this was happening right now. It had to be. She'd seen Martha's past up until the moment when they'd planned to kidnap her. She also knew they had rescheduled George's brain surgery for this evening.

Her heart beating fast, her breath coming in quick spurts, she edged closer. Closer still, then stopped and winced. At the base of George's head, they'd shaved his gray hair and removed a small portion of his skull. As Aiden used thin forceps, Martha kept squirting a clear liquid onto the exposed brain. Saline solution, Celeste supposed, to likely keep the organ from becoming dry.

"Almost there," Aiden said, glancing to the laptop which displayed a paused video of a brain surgery. "Yes. I believe this is it. Here's the Vein of Rosenthal, the culmen, and there's the pineal gland behind the third ventricle. See?"

Martha leaned over and cocked a brow. "Amazing. Excellent work. Now what?"

"Now we give the pineal gland an electric zap. While Dad believed electroshock helped awaken the pineal gland to some degree, he theorized that by giving the gland a direct hit, it would absorb the energy and completely open the *third eye*."

"But will George be able to handle a direct zap? I don't think he has a strong heart."

Aiden scooted the stool back to peer at George's face. "He's not awake. But we know he's alive." He grinned. "I think he fell asleep. That homemade anesthetic was a great idea. We couldn't have done the surgery without it."

"And I don't think we should be chatting when we have a man's skull opened and exposed," Martha said, setting aside the liquid she'd been squirting onto George's brain.

"Right. Sorry. I just can't believe *I* performed brain surgery."

Aiden reached behind him and brought up what looked like one of the electrodes he'd used for Celeste's electroconvulsive therapy, only this was a much smaller version and about the size of a Sharpie marker. "Dad wasn't sure how much voltage to use. I did some calculating based on his numbers, and I think we should go with the lowest possible. We want to shock the gland and awaken its power, not make George a vegetable."

Martha smiled and looked as if she was truly proud of her grandson. "You're the doctor, dear."

Aiden grew serious. He drew in a deep breath. Released it, then took in another.

"Okay, here we go," he said, pressing the electrode against the man's brain, then quickly taking it away.

George's body stiffened and bucked against the restraints around his back and legs. The man gasped and lifted his head from the massage pillow, revealing the shock in his wide eyes. The veins along his temples and neck bulged, his face turned red, then he fell against the pillow and stilled.

"What just happened?" Martha asked, her expression puzzled.

"I...I don't know. This should have worked." Aiden stood, then removed the man's restraints. He placed a large bandage over the opening along George's skull. "George, can you hear me?" he asked, and gently rolled the man on his back. He pulled a small flashlight from his pocket and pried one of George's eyelids open. "Grandma, check his blood pressure." As Martha wrapped the device around the man's upper arm, Aiden used a stethoscope to check his heart, then jerked back when George sat upright.

Both Martha and Aiden stared at him, alarm evident in their eyes.

"George?" Aiden went to his grandmother and moved her away from the man. "Can you hear me?"

George opened his eyes and looked around the room as if he were a blind man who'd just been given the gift of sight. The awe and wonder in his gaze, along with the huge smile brightening his face, almost made Celeste smile. Until he looked directly at her.

"Are you an angel?" he asked.

"Who's he talking to?" Aiden stepped away from his grandmother to face George. When the man kept his focus on Celeste, Aiden snapped his fingers. "George, look at me. Who are you talking to?"

"You can see me?" Celeste asked.

"I see through you. Are you a ghost? I've always been psychic, but I've never been able to see ghosts."

"I'm not a ghost. I'm being held in a room not far from yours. You need to stop talking to me and cooperate with Aiden and Martha. We have to find a way out of here."

"George," Aiden shouted, gaining the man's attention. "Who are you talking to?"

George cocked his head. "It's all so clear to me now." He burst into laughter and looked around the room. "So crystal clear. I can hear your thoughts. You're so confused and scared. My God." He drew in a deep breath. "You're a grown man, yet a simple boy who's been given a powerful intellect." He grabbed Aiden's arm, closed his eyes and shook his head. "Blood." Sadness crossed his face. "It didn't have to be this way."

Aiden jerked his arm away. "What are you talking about?"

"Your death."

"Enough," Martha shouted. "Stay away from him. Aiden, strap him to the bed until we figure out what's happening."

"What's happening is something beautiful." George smiled, but there was sorrow in his eyes. "I can see everything. And I can see you for what you really are. There's blackness around you." He turned toward Celeste. "Do you see it, too?" Pivoting he faced Martha again, then gripped her hand. "Oh, God." He quickly released her as if he'd been burned, then looked at his hand. "Not just blackness, but a void in your soul." George looked at Martha. "You're pure evil."

"I know what she's done," Celeste said. "Don't say anything else. If you want to survive, get back on the cot and be quiet."

"I can't be quiet. This is the best I've felt in years." He spread his arms and pulled in a deep breath. "God, I feel like I'm thirty again. But with a new perspective on life." George's gaze fell onto the equipment throughout the room. His brows drew together and he reached behind his head. "What did you do to me?" he asked as his fingers moved along the bandage and sank into the opening in his skull. "Oh my God! What did you do to me?"

"Restrain him," Martha yelled.

"No! Don't you touch me." George looked to the metal cart, where there was a small plastic container. "Is that part of my skull? Did you…" His face turned purple and he collapsed.

Celeste was torn from the room, and sent straight back to her prison. She opened her eyes and met Karen's ghostly gaze.

"What did you see?" Karen asked.

Celeste fought the nausea and fear. But she couldn't fight the tears. "How I'm going to die."

CHAPTER 7

Maxine Morehouse's Residence, Chicago, Illinois
Sunday, 8:07 a.m. Central Daylight Time

JOHN SAT NEXT to Olivia on the floor of Maxine's unicorn parlor, paper and crayons in front of his daughter. Once again, Ian was there, along with Hudson and Eden, who held Mason.

"Olivia, can you draw another picture for me?" Maxine asked.

Liv slipped her thumb into her mouth and crawled onto John's lap. She shook her head against his chest.

"She didn't sleep well," John explained. None of them had. Even Mason had woken up several times during the night.

"I see white an yellow girl," Olivia said around her thumb. "Her scare me."

John nudged her hand from her mouth. "She's not real."

"Uh-huh. Her like Edwart."

Maxine raised a silver brow. "Celeste has never mentioned any spirits in your house."

He had a strict rule: he refused to live with dead people. His wife loved their old home so much that John doubted she would tell him if any ghosts resided there. "Not to me, either. Liv started talking about the girl right after her bath last night, and that Celeste said to like her."

Olivia nodded. "Mommy say that."

"Okay, honey." John rubbed her arms. "Let's not talk about the girl. Let's see if we can find Mommy. Just like we did yesterday."

"Wif flying ponies?"

"That's right." When his daughter didn't respond, he lifted her until she faced him. "Listen to Daddy. I need your help. You're a big helper for Mommy all the time, right?"

She put her arms around his neck. "No big helper," she said with a pout.

"Olivia," Eden began, "if you help, you can leave with me. We'll pick up your cousin, Hannah, from Uncle Will's, then we'll all go to McDonald's. I'll get you a Happy Meal. And guess what? There'll be a My Little Pony inside."

His daughter's eyes brightened and a smile crossed her face. She immediately sat on the floor and picked up the purple crayon. "Livy love ponies."

When John looked to Eden, his sister-in-law shrugged. "When all else fails, don't be afraid to bribe," she said.

"Whatever works." He placed his hand over the one Olivia used to hold the crayon. "Okay, Liv, let's make a snowman like we did yesterday," he said, then began helping her draw a figure eight.

"Good girl," Maxine praised his daughter. "Keep watching the purple on the paper, and think about your Mommy and how much you want to see her."

Together he and Olivia drew on the paper, repeating the pattern over and over, layering the figure eight until it became thick and bold. Minutes passed. His daughter gasped as the thick purple eight rose from the page in a wide band and wrapped itself around his and Olivia's hands and wrists. "I see hole! I see!"

John stared at the paper, eagerness and anxiety tugging at his gut. "I see it, too."

"Be wary, John."

As the purple extended up their arms, and the room began to swirl with flying unicorns, John looked up at Edward. Behind him were the other ghosts. Like Edward, concern was etched on their faces. "Why?" John asked. "What do you know?"

"We fear what Miss Olivia might see. Your love for Celeste is strong, as it should be, but you must put your daughter's health first."

"Daddy, my belly hurt," she said, her eyes following the swirling unicorns.

"Look at the hole, not the ponies. We're almost there." He met Edward's gaze. "Remember, Daddy will protect you."

Edward and the other ghosts faded as the unicorns and purple bands created a tunnel. It narrowed, grew tighter, and at the center was a bright light. "Think about Mommy. Keep thinking about how much you love her," John encouraged, then he and Olivia were thrust forward and into blackness.

"I scared!"

"Ssh." John blinked several times. Once his eyes adjusted, the dark shadows revealed the corners of walls and a staircase. "Don't let go of my hand," he said, taking a step forward.

"John, where are you?" Maxine asked.

"I'm not sure. It's not the same place as yesterday." When he took a few more steps, light from beneath the crack under a door glowed along the floor. "I see a light," he said, walking them toward it. "There's a door here, but it's closed." He reached for the knob, but his hand fell right though it. "I can't get inside."

"Because you're not physically there. Walk through it. Celeste can do this, so Olivia should be able to as well."

He looked down at his daughter, and considered Edward's advice. "Liv, want to try a magic trick? You can only do this when you've gone into the hole, understand?"

"Uh-huh," Olivia let out a shaky grunt.

"I know you can count to ten, but let's count to three then walk into the door."

"Daddy, that silly," she said with a nervous giggle. "We bonk head."

"We won't. Come on, let's give it a try. Ready? One, two, three…"

They stepped through the closed door and into a bright room. Olivia immediately tried to pull her hand from him. "White an yellow girl!" She turned toward the door.

"Stop. I see her, too." John held his daughter firm and stared at a ghost, who was, as Olivia had insisted, pure white and surrounded by yellow, and hovering above a bed. "Don't be scared. Daddy's here. Just close your eyes. I promise, we won't stay long, then you can get McDonald's."

Once Olivia had closed her eyes, John led her toward the bed, then braced his knees before they buckled. Celeste lay there with her eyes closed, a thin blanket covering her waist and legs. A black strap had been wrapped over her chest and kept her secured to the bed. She didn't appear to be in any pain, and thankfully there were no bruises, cuts or signs of abuse to her face or arms.

"Look?" Olivia asked.

"Not yet. Keep holding my hand, but move behind me. No peeking, got it?"

With a nod, she stepped behind him. "White an yellow girl gone?"

"Yes," he lied to keep her calm and cooperative.

"Are you in the room?" Maxine asked.

"It's a basement," he said, then described the windows, the grass just outside the glass. "She's here."

"John, describe every detail," Ian said.

As he began, Celeste's eyes opened and she stared up at the ghost. She frowned, then shook her head. The ghost lowered herself closer to Celeste, the yellow surrounding her fluctuating in color, darkening to orange. Her pale face contorted with impatience, as if the two of them were having a mental argument.

"There's not much in the room," John finally said, moving them even closer to the bed. Aching to touch his wife, helpless and unable to cut away the restraints holding her, he cleared his throat to keep his voice steady and strong for Olivia's sake. "A cabinet, bed, dressers, water pitcher. No signs of who the house belongs to or where it's located."

"Can you get to the upper level where you saw the stack of mail?" Maxine asked.

John didn't want to leave Celeste, but knew the best way to help her was to search the house. "I'll try," he said, backing away from the bed. "Liv, keep your eyes closed for just another second. We're going to go back through the door." He quickly turned, blocking her from seeing Celeste and the ghost, then together they stepped through the door and into the shadows. "You can open your eyes now."

Olivia squeezed his hand tightly. "It dark."

"I know," he said going toward the stairs.

"Look! Light," she said, pointing in the opposite direction, where a dim light sliced through the hallway's shadows.

Hoping for an office, or the kidnappers themselves, John turned them away from the stairs. As they made their way toward the room, and John realized the door was open, he once again moved Olivia behind him, shielding her from whatever might be inside. Nervous energy worked through him as they stepped into the room, followed by revulsion.

On the floor lay a man on his stomach. The back of his head had been shaved and was covered with a bandage. Medical equipment was scattered throughout the room. Unease slithered up his spine. "Liv, close your eyes again," he said, then walked toward a table near the head of the cot. On it, and next to a closed laptop, was a hardback book titled, *The Human Anatomy*.

Dread had his skin crawling. He looked to the filthy scalpel and forceps resting on a metal cart, to the plastic container holding what looked like bone, then back to the man. This time, he focused on his profile, and recognized George Meadows from his driver's license photo.

With urgency and fear for Celeste, and what the couple might do to her, he rushed Olivia from the room. "You can open your eyes again," he said as they made their way to the steps. The door at the top of the staircase opened, the basement lights turned on, revealing other closed doors in the basement.

The man they'd seen yesterday whistled as he headed down the wooden steps. When he reached the bottom, he went to the room where George Meadows lay dead. Seconds later, he exited, pushing the metal cart. When he reached Celeste's room, he opened the door.

"Morning," he said, bringing in the cart. "Grandma decided to skip church today. After our breakthrough last night, we're both anxious to get started right away. Her friend picked up the muffins and blanket she'd made for the church sale."

"How nice of her," Celeste replied with heavy sarcasm.

"Mommy!" Olivia squealed at the sound of her mother's voice, and pulled at John's hand.

"Liv, no," he said, stopping her just outside of the room.

"I hear Mommy." She tugged hard and began crying. "I see her."

"Later, we have to go upstairs."

"No! I..."

Olivia stood very still. Her eyes grew round and filled with terror. John followed her gaze and swore under his breath. The white and yellow ghost hovered at the door, staring directly at Olivia. The ghost smiled and reached out her hand toward his daughter. Liv smiled, too, until Celeste spoke again.

"Mommy!"

The ghost became frantic, her yellow changing shades.

"What's happening?" Maxine asked when Olivia started bawling uncontrollably. *"Olivia is fighting to free her hand from yours."*

Not having time to register how Maxine would know this, John tugged at his daughter. "Hurry, honey. We need to go. We need to—"

He drew in a shaky breath and blinked several times. He looked down at his empty hand, then to his daughter, who cried against the area rug in Maxine's parlor.

"Damn it." He stood and pushed a hand through his hair. "I just needed a little more time," he shouted, unable to control his anger and impatience. Why couldn't Olivia have cooperated?

"I sorry," Olivia said on a sob, and slipped her hand in his. "Livy bad girl."

Guilt melted his anger. He dropped to a knee and pulled her close. "No, you're not. You did a good job today. Daddy's sorry for yelling." When she hugged him, he looked to Hudson.

His best friend and brother-in-law stood. "Eden, maybe you should take Liv to the kitchen for a snack."

"Yes," Maxine agreed. "There are plenty of things in the pantry and juice in the fridge."

With tears misting her eyes, Eden met John's gaze. "You saw her?" she asked, taking Olivia's hand.

"We saw white an yellow girl," Olivia announced. "Her say to like her."

"How?" John asked. "She didn't move her mouth."

Olivia pointed to her head. "Livy hear." Worry wrinkled her forehead. "I still good girl?"

"Of course." He kissed her cheek. "Go with Auntie E and get a snack."

Once they left the room, John sank onto the couch.

"What'd you see?" Hudson asked.

"A dead man," he said, then explained everything in detail.

Ian scrubbed a hand down his face, stood then went to the window. "Describe the ghost."

"Who cares about her?" John let his frustration surface. "We need to contact the FBI and—"

"And tell them what?" Ian faced him. "What are you going to say, John? That a psychic reading you did with your three-year-old has led you to believe an old woman and her grandson cut open a man's head?"

Fuck. The entire story sounded preposterous. "We have to do something before they hurt my wife." He looked to the parlor door. "I need Liv to take me back there."

A unicorn figurine fell from the mantel and shattered against the hardwood floor.

With anger lining her face, Maxine looked from the broken unicorn to John. "I don't think my ghosts like that idea." She rose and left the room, then returned right away with Olivia, a broom and dustpan.

Eden followed behind with Mason. "What broke?" she asked.

Maxine began sweeping up the glass. "My *white and yellow* unicorn. Olivia, is Edward here?"

"Uh-huh."

"Edward, explain why you broke my unicorn."

Olivia sat with Eden and Mason on the couch. "White an yellow girl impotent." She frowned. "Im*por*tant."

Maxine glanced over to John and raised a haughty brow. "Do you know who cares about ghosts? Your wife. And so do I. The spirit you saw *is* important. It sounds to me as if she was trying to help or protect Celeste. And I find it extremely intriguing that she was able to see and communicate with Olivia, when she wasn't physically there. Don't you realize the significance?"

He did, and if he wasn't so damned worried about Celeste, he might feel guilt. "The girl had very pale skin, milky-blue eyes and white hair."

"Like an albino?" Eden asked.

"Yes, and the yellow was more like a cloud that hung around her."

"Impossible." Ian walked across the room to kneel in front of Olivia. "You said the white and yellow girl talked to you in here." He touched the top of her blond head. "What did she say again?"

"Like her," Liv responded, and snuggled close to Eden.

Ian looked to Maxine, who stared at Olivia. "Olivia said the same thing last night after she saw the ghost, except *Celeste* told her, not the girl."

"Oh, my God." Maxine leaned the broom against the fireplace. "She's telepathic."

Hudson blew out an impatient breath. "Come the fuck on."

"Hudson!" Eden glared at her husband. "Little ears, remember?"

"Sorry, but seriously. Thanks to you guys, I believe in ghosts, possession and psychics, but telepathy? Lemme guess…next you'll tell me my niece is going to go all *Carrie* on us and start tossing things around the room with her mind."

The hint of a smile tilted Ian's lips as he pulled out his cell phone. "You barbaric, crude genius."

Hudson's brows rose. "Is that a compliment?"

"It is."

"Then do you want to let me know why?"

"You say you don't believe in telepathy or telekinesis. Thirty-five years ago, I met the parents of a young *albino* girl who had been murdered by Dr. Seth *Ryker*. John, do you remember the state where this took place?"

"Maryland." John stiffened as he recalled what he knew about the Ryker investigation. "*Ryker*," he said, glancing to Olivia. "*Like her*. She was trying to give us their last name."

"Except, Ryker is in prison," Eden reminded them.

"Can someone fill me in on who you guys are talking about?" Hudson asked.

"Seth Ryker abducted our mom when she was pregnant with Celeste," she said, then explained why Ryker had done it.

"Sick and creepy." Hudson nodded. "Okay, so we have a copycat then?"

"Maybe not." Ian placed a call, then held the phone to his ear. "Rachel," he began, "I need you to dig up what you can on Dr. Seth Ryker's mother and son. Mother's name is Martha, and the son is Aiden. Don't get caught up in the details. As soon as you find out if both are still alive, I need you to call me right away with their addresses."

"If it's the mom and son, it's been thirty-five years," Hudson said. "What would motivate them to go after Celeste? How would they know to go after her?"

When it comes to your wife, I might've given myself some added insurance.

John remembered what Vigo had told him after he'd confessed to snooping around Ian's office and discovering the files his father-in-law had on him, Celeste, Olivia and…Janice. That son of a bitch. He hoped to God the bastard suffered in Hell.

"Vigo," John said. Everyone looked at him, but he focused on Ian. "He saw your files, and read about Janice. He could've contacted them, or Dr. Ryker."

Ian's eyes filled with regret. "If that's the case, this is all my fault. Those were my files, Ryker was my enemy."

John shook his head. "No one is to blame except the people who chose to take my wife. Call your pilot and have him ready the jet. Once we have an address, I want to be in the air."

And if the Rykers had his wife, and harmed so much as a hair on her head, Martha and Aiden had better hope the FBI got to them first. Otherwise he'd make sure he had a justifiable reason to kill them.

The Ryker Residence, Silver Spring, Maryland
Sunday, 9:42 a.m. Eastern Daylight Time

A LOCK OF Celeste's blond hair dropped to the concrete floor. She didn't bother to resist. Moments ago, they'd put her on her stomach, then had strapped her to the bed again, leaving her no option but to cooperate. With her face nestled in the center opening of a massage pillow similar to the one she'd seen George lying on last night, the buzzing from the electric razor Martha used to shave her hair hummed through her head.

A tear dropped to the floor, landing on top of one of her curls. She didn't care about the hair. It would eventually grow back, but only if she survived. *But how?* How could she find a way to free herself before they Frankensteined her?

Last night, after she'd finished the horror movie that was Martha's life, and had returned to her room, she'd tried to figure out how she could use that knowledge against the woman. Nothing had come to mind except revulsion, hatred and fear. The old woman was a ruthless, cold-blooded bitch who took pleasure in causing other people pain.

Because she could.

When Martha had stopped by Celeste's room after George's surgery, the old woman had asked if Celeste had used the ladybug necklace to look into her past. Celeste had given the jewelry back to her without a word. After everything she'd seen, she hadn't been sure how to respond. For whatever reason, Martha had wanted Celeste to know what no one—except maybe Larry, the hospital orderly—had known. Had she wanted to scare Celeste? She'd told her earlier that she had wanted someone to know the truth, but why? What was the point? Bragging rights?

The buzzing ceased. Cool air touched along a small section of Celeste's scalp near the base of her skull. She turned her head to the side and met Martha's cruel gaze. "Are you enjoying yourself?" she asked.

"Immensely." The old woman ran a finger along the clean-shaven part of Celeste's scalp. "Are you talking to me now? You were very tight-lipped last night."

"Watching you murder people has that effect on me."

Martha smiled. She slipped her glasses from her nose and let them dangle from the chain. "What did you see?"

"Why does it matter? I am curious, though. I'm guessing the first vision of you was in the early '60s. You would've been in your thirties, right?"

"What was the vision?"

"You, prostituting one of your patients."

"There were many. Which one?"

Many? God, the woman was sick. "She banged her head against the wall."

Martha shrugged and rolled her eyes. "Girl, I worked in an asylum for the mentally ill. Do you know how many of those people did that?"

"You murdered her. While she was catatonic, you pinched her nose and held her mouth closed."

The old woman's wrinkles deepened along her forehead. She nodded. "Early '60s? That was probably Thelma. She was a head-banger. But so was that other gal. I can't remember her name. Anyway, tell me what else you saw."

"No. What I'm curious about is your life prior to the '60s. You said you're going to be eighty-six in October. Your son is what? Almost seventy?"

"He's sixty-nine. His father knocked me up when I was sixteen." Martha touched her fluffy white hair. "And died of an unfortunate accident when Seth was ten."

"You mean you killed him."

"He'd been working under our car when the jack gave way and crushed him." Martha gave Celeste a couple innocent blinks. "What's even more tragic is that my darling, Seth, found him."

"Is this the point where you want me to tell you that I think you're sick and twisted? Are you proud of that?"

"Honestly? I am." She leaned close, subjecting Celeste to her stale coffee breath. "No one but you knows what I've done. And I've done so many bad things. Yet I haven't been caught. Can you believe it? I've never even been suspected of any wrongdoing."

"Larry knew."

Martha's brows lifted. "Larry. I haven't thought of him in years. He committed suicide back in '81."

"You mean you killed him."

She shook her head. "Nope. Can't take credit for Larry. The stupid man had a thing for boys. He got caught, and ended up shooting himself in the head just before the cops came to arrest him." Martha sighed. "Which meant I no longer had anyone to help me get rid of bodies. So I quit Forest Haven. Seth's wife had left him, so I decided to stay home and help him raise Aiden."

Celeste put her face back into the massage pillow. "You killed Sally. Her ghost is in the coal room."

Pain shot across Celeste's scalp as Martha lifted her head by her remaining hair. "Are you lying?"

Celeste's eyes prickled with tears. "What good would it do me?"

She released Celeste's hair. "She's still, in a way, being tortured then?" Martha asked, her tone hopeful.

The woman had no soul. "When you die, what do you think will happen to you?"

Martha chuckled. "You psychic people are too wrapped up in

God, the universe and some higher power. This might surprise you, but I actually believe we're all recycled. We die, then we're born again, here on Earth. Hopefully in my next life I'll be born into a wealthy family. Imagine what I could do if I had money," she said with a sly smile.

Imagine what I would do if I had a gun.

The old woman's eyes widened. "You want to shoot me. I heard you." She picked up a syringe from the tray next to her. "You really are impressive. It'll be interesting to see what happens to you once Aiden gives your pineal gland a zap."

"I'll end up like George. Dead."

Martha shook her head. "I don't know. George was seventy-two and not in the best shape. You're young and healthy. The challenge will be surviving brain surgery." Martha held up the syringe. "Your doctor is finishing sterilizing his surgical tools, and will be in shortly. Unless you want to do this without any anesthetic, I suggest you put your face back in the pillow."

"How is it you have that?"

"The anesthetic? I made it. I found the recipe online." She grinned. "That same day I discovered a new muffin recipe, too. Now, head down."

Celeste's stomach twisted. "You don't have to do this."

"Celeste, dear heart, do you really think I can let you leave here alive?"

"But what if the experiment works?"

Martha bent close to her ear. "I'm still going to kill you." She narrowed her eyes. "Now, face back into the pillow."

"No," Celeste said, terrified that this was it. That she'd reached the point of no return, and her life would soon come to an end. What did she have to lose by defying the old bitch?

"Your children and husband." Karen hovered behind Martha. *"I told you. I saw your daughter. I told her the name, Ryker."*

Earlier, as Aiden had begun prepping her room for her *surgery*, Karen had become frantic, telling her that a little girl with blond, curly hair was there, crying and calling for her mommy. The ghost had insisted she *felt* that the girl was Celeste's daughter, and had described what Olivia looked like. While Karen had every detail right, and Celeste had wanted to believe her—and still wanted to—the ghost could also get inside her head, and might have seen an image of Olivia. Plus, Liv was three and didn't know how to do a reading.

I know you did, Celeste said, not wanting to doubt the girl or hurt her feelings. Karen had already been through so much, and was counting on Celeste to help finally free her.

Aiden stepped into the room carrying his surgical tools and wearing a smile.

The last shred of hope Celeste had been clinging to immediately disappeared. This was going to happen. These people were going to do to her what they did to George. They were going to open up her skull and kill her.

For the first time, the ghost's aura blackened. *"There has to be a way. We have to be free. I want to go to the light. If you die, we'll be stuck here."*

Celeste closed her eyes. *There is no way out of this. Martha is soulless and doesn't care who she hurts. And she controls Aiden.*

"I was here when Aiden talked about his father." Karen hovered over Aiden. *"He loves and respects him. You have to convince him this is wrong, and not what his father would want."*

But this was exactly what his father wanted. Ryker had been certain he could create super-spies, take a person without psychic abilities and give them the gift, or make a psychic even more powerful.

"Is she ready? Aiden asked.

"She will be soon," Martha said. "But she won't cooperate. Hold her head so I can inject her."

"Sure." He set the tray on the table, then he pressed Celeste's face into the pillow. "Stay still."

Panicking, terrified, she shook her head, then cried out when the needle pricked her scalp. "No! Please don't do this."

"Don't move or we'll have to strap down your head," Aiden

said, his grip tightening.

Karen's face appeared inches from hers. *"Fight."*

Celeste fisted her hands, held the ghost's gaze and pressed her head back.

Martha sighed. "If you keep it up, we'll knock you out with a hammer."

Celeste stilled and held Karen's worried gaze.

"Geez, Grandma. We don't have to do that."

"Do you really think you can perform surgery on a bobbing head?"

Aiden sighed. "Well, no. But hitting her seems *wrong*."

"Because it *is* wrong," Celeste said, once again lifting her head and refusing to cooperate. "Everything you're doing here is wrong. Just like it was when your father did this thirty-five years ago. You murdered a man. George is dead. And for what? To help free your dad who was *also* a murderer?"

"I told you, those deaths were accidental. Just like… How did you know George died?"

"I was there last night. I saw what happened. You sent electricity directly into his pineal gland."

Excitement brightened Aiden's eyes. "Oh, my God. He was talking to *you*. Remember Grandma? Remember how we were wondering if he was seeing ghosts, or if he'd just lost his mind?"

"I remember, dear."

"How is that possible?" Aiden continued. "Did you have an out of body experience?"

"I don't know how he saw me," Celeste said. "And it doesn't matter. What does is ending this now, before you kill me, too."

Aiden looked to his grandmother. "I'll get the hammer."

"Wait! Why?" Celeste panicked, and craned her neck. "Didn't you hear me?"

"Loud and clear. You just reinforced the purpose and importance of this experiment. René Descartes believed the pineal gland was 'the principal seat of the soul and the place in which all our thoughts are formed.' In many cultures and religions, the gland is also known as the *third eye*, and is considered to hold the powers of perception and intuition. My dad believed this to be true, and so do I. Think about this…George was psychic, but his gift was weak and nothing like yours. Yet after his surgery, after I *opened* his third eye with electricity, he could see things he couldn't before. Which means we've proved my father's theory right. We can take a person like George, and likely someone without any psychic ability, and either increase their power or turn them into a clairvoyant. Since your gift is already strong, I can't wait to see what you'll become once I open *your* third eye."

Celeste didn't want to be knocked unconscious. Should a miracle happen, and she had an opportunity to escape, she needed to be awake. Martha's homemade anesthetic was topical and would numb her flesh, not her mind. She hoped. "Please don't get the hammer. I'll cooperate," she said, placing her face back inside the pillow's donut hole.

"Smart girl," Martha said.

Karen moved until she and Celeste were almost nose to nose. *"I'm so sorry."*

When the needle pierced her skin, Celeste was too. She was sorry she couldn't free Karen, or any of the other ghosts trapped in the Ryker house. Sorry they would not receive their justice, and that she would die without exposing Martha's life-long murder spree. She had a beautiful, powerful gift, and, once again, it was useless. If anything, her gift was damaging, and had caused too much hurt—especially to her family.

"Why would you think that?" Karen asked, her eyes brimming with tears. *"Why are you being hard on yourself? None of this was your fault."*

Please stay out of my head. Celeste closed her eyes. *You don't understand. I set this all in motion.*

"Vigo? The man who told Aiden and Martha about you?"

Yes. I accidentally set him free. From there, he nearly destroyed my marriage, almost killed my husband, and now… Celeste's tears passed through the ghost as they dripped to the floor. *I don't want to die. I need more time. I need to kiss my babies, watch them grow and mature into adults, then hold and love the grandchildren they'll give me. And my husband... John will blame himself for not being able to help me. He's such a good man. I wish I could tell him I love him, feel his arms around me just one last time.*

"Are we ready?" Aiden asked.

"Her scalp should be numb enough," Martha replied. "Just in case, I think we should strap down her head."

"You're probably right."

"Please don't," Celeste begged, when Aiden began strapping her head in place. "Please, please, please." Tears dripped from her face and clogged her throat. Her stomach cramped and grew nauseated. Her heart raced, pounded hard. Her ears rang, her head buzzed with fear.

"Here we go," Aiden said, as the tip of a sharp object touched Celeste's scalp.

"I can feel that!" She froze, didn't move a muscle. "The anesthetic didn't work."

"I gave her the same amount as George," Martha said. "Do we have more? It'd be in George's room."

"Let me check."

Once Aiden's footfall grew distant, Martha leaned close to Celeste's ear. "There isn't any more," she whispered. "And I only gave you a quarter of the dosage you need. I want to watch you suffer."

God, she hated this woman. Wanted Martha dead. Would love to watch as every person Martha had harmed tore at the old woman's flesh and muscle, ripped apart her limbs and smashed her skull.

Blackness, unlike anything Celeste had ever experienced, filled her core, her heart and head. A dark energy moved through her. She met Karen's pale gaze. The girl studied her as if seeing Celeste for the first time. Then a slow smile curved the corners of her mouth.

"There isn't any more," Aiden said, returning to the room.

"And we don't have any more Lidocaine Hydrochloride left to make another batch."

"Then we do without." Martha tested the straps along Celeste's head. "We had to order the drug from one of those online stores, and it took a week for it to get here. We don't have a week, not if people are looking for her."

"True." Metal scraped along metal, and Celeste pictured Aiden picking up the scalpel. "Should we gag her?"

"No." Martha's gnarled fingers brushed Celeste's arm. "Let her scream until she passes out."

CHAPTER 8

"I HATE YOU," Celeste said, welcoming the dark energy and letting it consume her. "Your own son wants you dead. Aiden, aren't you the least bit curious why?"

"Grandma explained it to me. My dad only said that because he was scared for me. He doesn't want me to end up in prison like him."

"It's more than that." Celeste fisted her hands. "Martha was the one who called the FBI on your father. It's because of her he got caught and is now spending life in a state penitentiary."

"Don't be ridiculous. Stop talking or we will gag you," Aiden said. "I can't concentrate if you keep trying to get in my head."

Karen's aura brightened. *"Yes, get in his head. Try it. Show him what his grandmother has done."*

I don't know if I can. Celeste honestly didn't, not only because she wasn't sure if she could communicate mentally with a living person, but her mind had become clouded with hatred and rage. Her body tingled and vibrated with it. *I can't pull my thoughts together.*

Aiden touched her head. "Now, don't move," he ordered.

Celeste screamed. Jerked against the restraints as pain burned a path along her scalp. She let out another long wail when her head was pressed against the pillow and Aiden proceeded to cut her.

Her vision blurred into tiny dots of color. She blinked them away, only to have the dots replaced with worm-like floating strings. As her stomach cramped, then balled up, the strings clumped together, creating images of Martha. Images and the sounds of things she hadn't seen during the reading. Faces contorted in pain. Blood. Bruised flesh. People crying in misery. Decaying bodies in a grave.

"We just need to pin back her skin, then I can remove the bone," Aiden said, his voice tinny, distant.

Terror pierced Celeste's belly as she stiffened and gasped from the excruciating agony ripping at the back of her head. The ball in her stomach tightened. Coiled. Her fingers and toes tingled. Fear rushed through her veins, spread, splintered and collided with her hatred as more horrifying images floated in her vision.

Let her scream...

Outrage suddenly outshined her fear. *How dare the bitch?*

Metal rattled against metal.

Who the fuck is she to decide my fate?

The lamp near Celeste's head swayed, then clanked against the floor.

They can't do this to me. They have no right to abuse my body, to tear me away from my family.

The cart holding the surgical tools crashed onto the concrete. The bloody scalpel skidded to a halt when it hit the cinder block wall.

"What's happening?" Aiden asked, his voice shaky, scared.

Celeste stared into Karen's eyes. Remembered every detail, every ounce of pain the girl had endured. *They should have never touched you.*

Celeste's hatred intensified. The metal cabinet groaned as it collapsed against the ground. The door slammed shut and the lights flickered.

"It's her," Martha shouted. "She's doing this."

"What?"

"I've seen it before. Forget the surgery. Kill her!"

"I don't want to kill her," Aiden whined. "It's not right."

Celeste smelled and tasted Aiden's fear. It made her hungry, made her want more from him.

"Focus on the straps," Karen encouraged her. *"Not Aiden."*

She wanted to destroy Aiden. Rot his brain. Leave him as nothing but an empty shell.

"Celeste! Listen to me. You're doing this with your mind. Focus on the straps. See them tearing apart."

Karen's frantic voice penetrated through the haze of hatred fogging Celeste's mind. *Impossible. You're doing this.*

The ghost shook her head and smiled. *"It's you. Don't stop! Focus on the straps. On your rage. On your babies waiting for you at home."*

Celeste couldn't think of her kids when she had murder and vengeance on her mind. Instead, she focused on the energy pooling at her core and then moving throughout her body. Pictured the fluorescent light above her. Closed her eyes and saw the glass, saw the atoms creating the gas within the glass cylinder, the electrical current running through it. Poured her energy into the current.

"I've raised another damned pussy," Martha said with disgust. "Get me the scalpel."

Celeste ignored the old woman. The hairs all over her body rose as she kept her focus on the light.

"I won't do it." Aiden rushed to the corner of the room where he'd left the old electroshock machine. "We'll stop her with shock therapy."

"No," Celeste yelled.

The fluorescent lamp shattered.

Aiden lurched back, his eyes rounding with shock. "Grandma, get out of here. Hurry!"

Celeste consumed the fear radiating from Aiden, concentrated on the fibers making up the straps binding her to the bed. Absorbed them, saw them shredded, splitting in two. The one across her head snapped, followed by the bands along her back and legs. While Aiden yelled out to his grandma again, she rolled to her side and caught Martha hurrying for the door.

Celeste looked at the hinges, imagined the metal moving, and slammed it shut.

The old woman turned and pressed her back against the door. "You don't scare me."

Celeste stepped onto the floor. Glass cut into her soles and heels, but she relished the pain, how it reminded her that she was alive and in total control. She picked up one of the scalpels that had fallen to the floor. "I should," she said, walking across the glass.

"Leave Grandma alone," Aiden shouted, and rushed toward her.

Celeste's feet slipped on her own blood as she darted for Martha. She grabbed the old woman, twisted her around and held the blade to her neck. "Don't move," she said, staring at Aiden. "Or I'll kill her. Who has the key?" When no one answered her, she pricked Martha's thin skin.

"Don't!" Aiden held up his hands and looked to his grandma, who pathetically whimpered. "I have it." He pulled the key from his pocket. "I'll bring it over."

Karen hovered behind him and shook her head. *"Don't trust him."*

"Trust me, I don't."

Aiden frowned. "Don't what?"

"I wasn't talking to you. I was talking to Karen Webber, the girl your grandma and dad killed after they'd removed part of her brain. She's right behind you."

Aiden slowly turned. "I don't see anything."

"Don't listen to her," Martha said. "And don't give her the key."

"That's fine." Celeste nicked her again. "I'll kill you, then kill him. At this point, I don't care if either of you lives. All I know is, I'm getting out of here."

Aiden pulled the key from his pocket and held it for Celeste to see. "Please don't hurt her. She's all I have."

"Toss it."

Instead of a gentle toss, Aiden threw the key in the opposite direction. With her mind clear and sharp, Celeste instantly honed in on it, stopped the key with her thoughts, smiled as she turned it and brought it toward her. "You people made a terrible mistake bringing me here," she said, amazed by the power she now held. "I learned a new trick." She snatched the key, then shoved Martha toward the bed.

The old bitch grunted as she caught herself. Then rested her rear on the mattress. "What are you going to do?" she asked, slipping on her glasses.

Vengeance burned through Celeste. "I'm going to destroy your family." She looked to Aiden. "Your grandma isn't the sweet muffin-baking, blanket-making old lady you and everyone around her seem to think she is. Your father didn't *accidentally* kill people in the name of science. He murdered them for his own selfish gain. And you..." A small amount of empathy weaseled its way into her heart. "You never had a chance, did you? Would you like to know why?"

"Aiden," Martha began, "don't listen to her."

Celeste smiled. "No worries. I don't plan on talking. I'm going to show him what you've done. Guess who learned another new trick?"

Hoping she actually could put ideas and images in his mind, Celeste focused on Aiden. She concentrated on Martha's past, on every gory detail, and even showed Aiden what his father had done to Karen, and how Martha had deceived her son.

Aiden's eyes rolled back. He staggered to the wall and leaned against it. After blinking several times, he glared at his grandmother, betrayal narrowing his eyes. "You killed my mother."

Martha straightened. She slid her gaze to Celeste, before looking to her grandson. "She was in the way of your father's dream."

"My father...you called the FBI on him. He's in prison because of you."

"He's in prison because he's a fool. The albino's parents were hounding him, threating that if Seth didn't produce their daughter, they were going to the police." She shook her head. "Then he stupidly kidnapped Janice. I figured either the police or the FBI would come knocking on our door, so I did what I had to do."

"Does he know you murdered my mother?"

"Don't know. Don't care." She wagged a finger at him. "Now quit your whiny belly-aching and go take care of Celeste. Unless you want to join your father in prison, we can't let her leave."

"Why would you do it?" Aiden asked as if he hadn't heard her. His hand trembled as he wiped his forehead. "Any of it? All those people." His face distorted with confusion and disgust. "How many people have you killed?"

Martha shrugged. "I'm not sure."

"Bullshit. You keep track of how many bowel movements you have in a week. I guarantee you know."

The old woman chuckled. After a moment, she sobered. "If I include the five I helped your father kill, and George, I'm sitting at fifty-nine." She glanced to Celeste. "I was hoping blondie would've helped me round out that number to sixty."

Aiden's shoulders slumped as he looked to the floor. "My God." He went to one of the stools, then sat and held his head in his hands. "My God," he repeated.

"Pray to God later. Come on, boy. Get up and get rid of her."

"Why?" he asked.

"Why get rid of her? I already told you."

"No." He stared at Martha. "Why did you do it?"

"Because she can," Celeste said, reaching for the doorknob.

Martha scooted off the bed. "Stop her!"

Aiden shook his head. "I can't." Tears filled his eyes. "This...everything we did here was wrong. I believed in my father. You made me believe in his work." He met Celeste's gaze. "I...I read about his experiments, but *seeing* what he did..." His face crumpled as he let out a sob. "That poor girl." He wiped his wet cheeks. "And I'm no better. I killed a man, and I can't take it back. All I wanted was to have my dad home." He cried harder. "That's all I've ever wanted." He quickly stood, toppling the stool backward, and pointed at his grandmother. "Not anymore. I'm not going to stop her. I'm going to stop *us*. You're a murderer, so is my father, and now I'm one, too. We all deserve to be in prison."

"Fool." Martha removed her glasses and glared at him. "I'm eighty-five. How many years do you think I'll be behind bars? But you, on the other hand, are a young man. Do you want to end up like your father and spend the next thirty-five years of your life in prison?"

Aiden looked to Celeste. "There's a phone in the kitchen."

With a final glance to Karen, who hovered next to Martha, scowling at the old woman with disdain, Celeste opened the door. She quickly shut, then locked it. As she rushed up the stairs, pain shot from the soles of her feet where she'd cut them on the glass. Her head also hurt, and warm blood trickled from the slice along the back of her head down her neck and into the opening of the hospital gown. By the time she'd reached the top step, she was dizzy and breathing hard. She opened the door, immediately spotted the phone hanging from the kitchen wall and limped to it.

The backdoor flew off its hinges. Startled, scared, Celeste turned just as uniformed officers, along with men and women wearing the FBI logo rushed inside, their guns raised and ordering her to get on the floor. Celeste dropped the scalpel and quickly complied, while other officers came in from the opposite direction. "My name is Celeste Kain," she shouted, and lay on her stomach. "Martha and Aiden Ryker kidnapped me."

One of the FBI agents touched her shoulder, then yelled for an EMT. "Sorry, ma'am," he said, lifting her into a seated position. "I'm Agent Dickenson. Are you okay? Can you tell us where they are?"

She winced when she pulled herself to her feet. "Follow me. I need to show you what they've done."

When the agent's gaze dropped to the bloody trail she'd left across the floor, he stopped her. "Stay here. You need medical assistance."

"No, I have to show you." She wanted to see if Karen had

gone, and be certain that the girl was finally free. "Please. I *need* to do this."

Agent Dickenson lifted her into his arms, while several other agents and officers either headed down the basement steps or to other parts of the house. "How did you know?" she asked the officer.

"Your husband."

Tears pricked her eyes. *John.* She didn't bother to ask whether John was here. If John had been, he would've been the first through the door. God, she couldn't wait to see him, fall into his arms and put this behind her. Except, she knew that wouldn't be possible. Not because of the things she'd seen or what had been done to her, but because of what she had become and the power she now held. She didn't even want to think about how John was going to react to her new talents.

When they reached the bottom, Celeste handed one of the officer's the key. "They're both in there." She pointed toward the opened door down the hall. "You'll find George Meadows in that room. They killed him last night."

The officer inserted the key into the lock. "Are they armed?"

She thought about the scalpel on the floor. "I've never seen them with a gun, but there's surgical equipment in the room. For sure, a scalpel."

He nodded, looked to the agent next to him, who raised her gun, then he turned the key. The female agent kicked in the door. Still holding Celeste, Agent Dickenson stayed behind while the rest of the team flooded the room.

"What the...?" one man said.

Celeste squirmed until Agent Dickenson gently set her down, then she drew in a steadying breath when her battered feet screamed in protest. Following behind Agent Dickenson, she entered the room. Karen hovered near the corner, where Aiden sat against the wall, blood pooling onto his shirt from the gash along his throat. Holding a bloody scalpel, Martha sat beside him, blood-spatter along her snow-white hair, face, glasses and clothes.

Celeste met the old bitch's cold gaze. Martha smiled. "And that makes sixty," she said, tossing the blade to the floor.

As the officers hauled Martha to her feet and cuffed her, Karen, whose aura was now as white as her skin and hair, moved toward Celeste. She gave Celeste a big grin. *"God didn't forget me."* The girl's body grew faint. *"You're so special. I believe you were brought here for a reason. Maybe it was to save me, or maybe it was to help you realize your true potential. Either way, I hope you realize the beauty of your gift. Thank you, Celeste,"* she said, then disappeared.

Her gift, her new abilities were amazing. Celeste didn't understand why she'd been blessed with them, but wondered if her gift had been given to her for a bigger purpose. What that might be, she had no clue. Too tired to think, relieved the ordeal was finally over, and needing to get out of the officers and agents' way, she stepped back into the hallway.

Five more white figures glowed in the shadows. As they neared her, she recognized George, who nodded to her. "Thank you," he said, slowly fading to nothing.

Aiden's mother, Sally, came next and offered her gratitude before dissolving away. More of Dr. Ryker's victims followed behind. Oscar Martinez, Thomas Hill and Holly Simon also thanked her, then vanished.

Two EMTs came down the steps, then carried her back to the kitchen, where a stretcher waited. As they checked her vitals and prepared her for the ambulance ride, another spirit entered the room.

Darla? Celeste asked. Hoping this was Darla Kemper, the woman who could see into the future, and Dr. Ryker's third victim. She also hoped there were no other spirits in the house—courtesy of Martha.

The woman came closer. *"Yes. Nurse Martha will go to prison as I knew she would."*

Too bad she's so old, Celeste said, then winced when one of the EMTs placed gauze against the wound along the back of her head. *I'd like to see her suffer for a long time.*

Darla smiled. *"Before I was murdered, I told Martha her grandson would die young and violently, and that her son would die by his own hand. I also told her she would live past one hundred, but that she needn't fear dementia or Alzheimer's disease."* Her smile grew. *"She will know what it is like to suffer."* The woman began to fade. *"Thank you,"* she said, then evaporated.

Later, when Celeste was being hoisted into the ambulance, she stared at the front door of the Ryker residence. Sick satisfaction warmed her as the police and FBI walked Martha from the house and to a squad car. Aiden's gray spirit floated behind the old woman, and followed her into the cruiser. Once inside, Aiden turned, met Celeste's gaze and smiled.

"I will haunt her all the way to Hell," he said, just as the EMTs closed the ambulance's doors.

Holy Cross Hospital, Silver Spring, Maryland
Sunday, 1:12 p.m. Eastern Daylight Time

WITHOUT WAITING FOR Hudson, Dante or Ian, John got out of the rental car and ran inside the hospital. The hour and forty minute flight had been hell. After the FBI had contacted them and said they'd found Celeste alive with no life-threatening injuries, he'd been unable to do anything but spend the entire flight worrying.

Years ago, he'd met and had fallen hard for her during an investigation. She'd been taken then, too. But the worry and anxiety he'd dealt with during that time had been nothing compared to the devastation, the helplessness he'd endured since she had been kidnapped from the hotel. His love for her was now stronger. They'd made a life together, had children to consider.

After checking a map on the wall, he bypassed the elevator and rushed up three flights of stairs. Once he reached the third floor and found Celeste's room, a uniformed officer stopped him.

"I'm John Kain. My wife is in there."

"Let him in," a man opened the door. "I'm Agent Ike Dickenson. We spoke on the phone earlier."

John shook the man's hand, even though he wanted to shove him aside and go to Celeste. "Thank you for getting her out of there," he said, looking over the agent's shoulder and only seeing the foot of a hospital bed.

"Celeste did that on her own." Agent Dickenson stepped aside. "She's been asking for you."

Without hesitation, John went into the room and straight to the bed. Celeste was propped against several pillows, her blond curls framing her face. Her skin glowed, and she looked surprisingly radiant and well rested for someone who'd been abducted, drugged and tortured. When she smiled and held out her hand, relief weakened his knees. Love and concern had his heart tripping. He took her hand, sat on the edge of the bed and kissed her.

"I love you," he said, his throat tightening. "I was so scared." He touched his forehead to hers. "I'm sorry I couldn't get to you. I tried. I…" Frustration balled in his gut. There was so much to say, but he couldn't think straight with all the emotions pulling his thoughts in a million different directions.

"John, look at me." Celeste ran her fingers along his shoulder as he met her gaze. "I'm fine. They did hurt me, but they didn't break me. If anything, I'm stronger."

The intense confidence in her eyes made him proud. Celeste was a fighter, not a quitter. Instead of playing the role of a victim, she acted as if she'd just kicked ass on the battlefield. "You did good, baby." He kissed her again. "I want to know everything that happened." He fingered one of her curls. "Agent Dickenson told me they…" He clenched his jaw to keep his emotions in check. "That they…cut you."

She leaned forward. "I'm going to have to either get extensions or a new hair style," she said, turning her head to show him the bandage along the shaved part of her scalp.

Fury clawed at his gut, along with fear. Dickenson had told them what the Rykers had done to George Meadows. If Celeste hadn't found a way to escape, they would've done the same to her.

"I hate them. Aiden isn't dead enough. Martha should be, and Dr. Ryker needs to be held accountable for what they've done."

"Don't waste your energy on those people." Celeste leaned back into the pillows. "It's over. The doctor said I could leave tomorrow. I'm anxious to get home and see the kids. How are they?"

"It's not over. There'll be a trial. You'll be forced to relive what they did to you."

"I gave the FBI an account of what happened, and they found Martha holding the scalpel she'd used to slice Aiden's throat." Celeste half shrugged. "I doubt there will be a trial, but if there is one, I have no problem telling a jury what they did to me."

A knock came at the door. Agent Dickenson stepped inside the room. "Your father is here."

"Hudson and Dante came, too," John said.

"I want to see them." She took John's hand and pulled him toward her. "What I'm going to tell them is the version I gave the FBI," she whispered, excitement brightening her eyes. "I'll tell you the *whole* truth when we're alone."

"Is it something bad?"

Her grin was conspiratorial. "No, it's something wonderful."

She gave his hand a squeeze, then smiled when her dad and the others entered the room. After they'd all greeted her, she began explaining what had happened during her stay with the Rykers, about the electroconvulsive therapy, and how Martha and Aiden had planned to continue with Dr. Ryker's experiments in order to help shorten his prison sentence.

"They picked George Meadows because they knew he was psychic," she said.

Hudson leaned against the ledge near the window. "I wonder how they knew."

"George had actually volunteered to be involved with Dr. Ryker's original experiments. Fortunately for him, a death in the family forced him to postpone those plans. Otherwise he probably wouldn't have lived another thirty-five years. Unfortunately,

Martha remembered him."

"Why wasn't she arrested back then?" Dante asked. "I read the Ryker case file. There was little mention of her, but she had to have known what was going on in her own house."

Ian sat in the chair near the hospital bed. "Dr. Ryker claimed he forced his mother to help him. Martha said the same. And Janice also stated that the woman hadn't acted like a willing participant. Even though many of us believed Martha had a bigger role in the experiments and murders, we had no evidence to contradict this, so we let her go." He leaned back. "We always believed she was the one who turned Ryker in, but she never admitted it."

"She most definitely participated," Celeste said. "I was able to perform a reading on her. Martha was a very bad woman."

She spent the next twenty minutes telling them about Martha's time at Forest Haven, how the woman killed her daughter-in-law, her participation in Dr. Ryker's experiments and how she and Aiden planned her own kidnapping.

"Did you tell Agent Dickenson any of this?" Ian asked.

She shook her head. "None of it could be corroborated. Anyone who knew what Martha did there is dead. And I don't believe her son was aware of what she did while working at Forest Haven, or that she killed his wife." She sighed. "And it's not as if psychics make good courtroom witnesses."

Dante folded his arms across his chest. "The woman won't be punished long enough. How old is she?"

"Eighty-five. But one of the ghosts at the house told me Martha will live well past one hundred," Celeste said with a smile. "So there's that."

"The yellow and white ghost?" Hudson asked.

Celeste frowned. "Not her, Darla Kemper. How did you know about Karen?"

"Olivia." John gave her hand a gentle squeeze, then told her about the readings he'd done with their daughter. "We saw you and Karen this morning. If it wasn't for Karen and what she'd said to Liv, I don't know that we would've put it together that the Rykers had you."

Celeste's lips curved into a wistful smile. "Karen was a very special person. Our daughter is, too."

When a nurse came into the room to check Celeste's vitals, Ian kissed his daughter's forehead. "We're going to let you rest. We'll have plenty of time to talk during the flight home tomorrow."

John had no intention of leaving Celeste's side. At this point, he was seriously considering have GPS chips surgically implanted in her and their kids. There was no way he ever wanted to live through something like this again.

After the nurse left, he pulled a chair near Celeste's bed. Now that he'd seen her, and they'd had a chance to talk, he was calmer and able to pull his thoughts together. "How do you feel about Olivia performing a reading?"

"It makes me nervous. What if she starts drawing on paper and does one on her own?"

He hadn't thought about that. "Maybe we should get rid of every crayon and marker we own."

Celeste gave him a wry grin. "Or maybe Maxine and I should mentor her."

"Not until we've had a talk with her and Ian."

"Because?"

The curiosity and concern in Celeste's gaze had John regretting saying anything about Maxine and Ian. Celeste had been through enough today. He shouldn't pile on more, but he also wanted her to know that something wasn't right, that her father and her mentor were keeping secrets.

"Why don't you nap and we can talk about it later?"

"I'm not tired." She raised a brow. "Start talking."

He cleared his throat. "Are you thirsty?"

She pinched his arm. "Stop stalling and talk."

Knowing his wife, she would hound him until he gave her what she wanted. "Fine. Olivia is telepathic," he said, then explained what had happened at the hotel, how Karen had communicated with their daughter, and that Olivia had claimed both Ian and Maxine had a secret regarding Janice.

Celeste's eyes filled with worry. "I'm sure Ian has a ton of secrets. As for Maxine... When I was performing a reading on Aiden, he'd mentioned her to his father. Dr. Ryker gave me the impression he knew Maxine. But why didn't she tell me?" She shook her head. "Liv must've misunderstood."

"Wait, you're more surprised about Maxine than you are about Olivia?"

Celeste dropped her gaze to the blanket covering her waist.

He touched her chin, forcing her to look at him. "You knew?"

"No. I would've told you." Tears shimmered in her eyes. "I told you something special happened... John, I saw my mother. After they gave me electroconvulsive therapy, I was down and ready to give up and die. Karen tried to encourage me to fight, but I'd lost hope. The ghost entered my body, and she somehow took me back in time. She wanted me to experience what she'd gone through so I could find a reason to fight."

"Is that when you saw Janice?"

She nodded. "And much more. I discovered my mom was telepathic, just as Karen was."

"Could you communicate with your mom?" he asked, concerned with how this had impacted Celeste emotionally. She loved her mom, and he knew her loss still cut deep.

"No, and I'm okay with that. My mom wouldn't have known who I was, even if I could have talked to her. Still, it was something special seeing her."

John took her hand. "I'm sure it was, but are you upset she never told you she was telepathic?"

"I probably should be, since I discovered I am, too."

Oh, shit. John blew out a breath. He didn't know what to say or how to react. Talking to dead people had been one thing, but being able to talk with her mind? "Can you read my thoughts?"

"I haven't tried, and I wouldn't do that to you. I certainly wouldn't want you in my head, either. It's an invasion of privacy."

"It might come in handy when Olivia starts dating," he said, trying to make light of something extremely heavy. "We'll know what the boys are thinking."

She half smiled. "John, I'm being serious. I promise, I won't read your thoughts or plant ideas in your head." Her lips thinned into a grim line. "There's one more thing."

He rubbed a hand along his brow. "Bigger than telepathy?"

She nodded, and looked to the cup on the hospital tray near her bed. "Watch."

When the straw lifted from the cup, then spun in the air, John stilled. Goose bumps rose along his skin. "Did...ah..." He swallowed hard, stared at the twirling straw and tried to digest what he was seeing. "Is there a ghost in the room?" he asked, hoping that was the answer. But he suspected otherwise. Detective Dickenson had said the room where Celeste had been held looked as if a small explosion had been detonated in it. The lights had been shattered, the cabinet and cart had been thrown to the floor, and the restraints they'd used on Celeste had been shredded. And, according to Ian, Karen had allegedly been telekinetic.

"No ghosts. I'm doing this," she said as the straw dropped back into the cup.

"How? Can Olivia do that too?" he asked, looking at the cup again. "Did your mom have this power? Did you—"

"John, stop," Celeste said with a chuckle. "Slow down and let me explain. I don't think my mom was telekinetic, and neither is Olivia. When Karen took me back thirty-five years ago to experience what she'd gone through, she had a telekinetic episode and tore up the room. Dr. Ryker lied to her, and told her that her parents were afraid of her and no longer wanted her. I heard and felt her thoughts. The anger and betrayal were too overwhelming for her to handle. There was so much dark energy moving through her, and Karen wasn't a dark soul. She was a sweet, kind person."

A tear slipped down her cheek. "She couldn't control that energy, and blew out the windows, the light, knocked over furniture.

And…I think when she had this episode, she left a telekinetic imprint on me. That's the only explanation that makes sense." Celeste pulled the blanket toward her chest. "Because I did the same thing Karen did. The moment Aiden cut my scalp, the same dark energy moved through me. I didn't control it, didn't even know I was the one knocking over things until Karen told me." She took the tissue John offered her and wiped her eyes. "I don't know what to feel or think about being telekinetic. With the way you're looking at me, I'm guessing you're not sure what to do with this, either."

He had no clue. For fuck's sake, his wife could not only talk to the dead, but she could now get into peoples' heads and move objects with her mind. That scared him because, if the wrong people knew, or she was in a situation where she couldn't control the dark energy, she could hurt herself or others. And yet, he couldn't help being a little turned on by it all. His woman was a total badass.

He rose from the chair and sat on the bed. "I love you." He cupped her cheek. "Everything about you."

"But?"

"No buts." He smiled. "Well, maybe a few. Celeste, this scares the hell out of me. What if there are other Dr. Rykers out there? What if you lose control of this…power?" *What if you decide you don't need me?* Damn it. He couldn't admit that to her. He was supposed to be her rock. The person who kept her grounded.

He didn't want to confess his insecurities, or look like less of a man in her eyes. But after everything they'd been through, after what the Rykers had done to her, he owed it to her to be honest.

"Before you answer," he began, "I want you to get in my head and hear my thoughts."

Confusion crossed Celeste's pretty face. "I don't want to. Say what's on your mind. That's how it's always been between us and always should be." She leaned forward and gripped the front of his shirt. "Say it. You've never had a problem speaking your mind before, why should I have to read it now?"

He grasped her shoulders. "You're so damned special. I'm scared you don't need me."

"What are you talking about?" Her eyes glistened with tears and love. "Just because I can do things you can't doesn't mean I don't need you in my life. Besides, who else would put up with me?" She tugged him closer, bringing their lips only inches apart. "I love you. I don't ever want to be without you. And I need you more than ever. These new things I can do, they scare me, too. But knowing I have you eases my fears." She kissed him. "You know Olivia is like me. I think Mason is, too. We need one person in our lives who won't judge us and who will always keep us grounded. You vowed for better or for worse." She grinned. "I'm holding you to it."

God, he loved her. His insecurities forgotten, he leaned in for another kiss. "I'm not going anywhere without you or the kids. But if things start flying around the room the next time we have an argument, I'm bringing out the big gun."

"And that would be?"

He glanced toward his crotch. "Has it been that long?"

"Oh, my God. Really? Now?"

"Sorry, I couldn't resist." He grinned, then kissed her again. "I can't wait to take you home. The kids are going to be excited to see you. Especially Olivia. I'm worried about the things she's seen during the readings."

"I am, too. I'm also concerned about this secret she knows. Now that I think about it, it's a little too coincidental that she mentioned my mother's name, and that Dr. Ryker knew Maxine." Celeste leaned back into the pillow. "When we get home tomorrow, I want to get together with Maxine and Ian."

"Wait a few days. You've already been through enough."

She shook her head. "I'm tired of secrets."

"What if they don't want to tell you?"

Celeste smiled. "Then I'll make them tell me."

John chuckled and shook his head.

Yeah, his wife was a total badass.

CHAPTER 9

Two days later…
John and Celeste's house, Chicago, Illinois
Tuesday, 10:05 a.m. Central Daylight Time

MAXINE HUGGED CELESTE tightly. "I was so worried," she said, her voice shaky. She pulled back and brushed tears from her face. "How are you feeling?"

"I'm fine." Celeste led her mentor into the living room, where John sat on the couch, and Ian on the recliner. Ruth lay on the floor near where Olivia played with her toys, while Mason sat on Ian's lap, drooling all over a colorful set of plastic toy keys. "Would you like coffee?" she asked.

When John and Ian declined, and Maxine didn't answer, Celeste turned. Her friend's eyes filled with fresh tears. "Your head. Ian told me what they did to you, but… My God, darling." She hugged Celeste again. "I'm so sorry this happened to you."

Celeste directed her to the couch. "It's over. What's important is that I'm fine, and these people can't hurt anyone else."

"Absolutely." Maxine sat next to John and gave his forearm a squeeze. "Everything's good?"

John smiled and looked to Celeste. "Excellent."

And they were. As soon as they'd come home, Olivia had jumped into Celeste's arms and had started talking about the white and yellow girl, the purple that ate her arm, and Miss Santa Claus. Celeste had been waiting for her daughter's face to turn blue, considering Liv had barely stopped talking long enough to take a breath. Mason had let loose his pterodactyl scream the moment he'd seen her. Then he'd babbled up a storm, as if he had plenty to say about her being gone.

Later that evening, after everyone was bathed and having family snuggle time on her and John's king-sized bed, Celeste had asked Olivia about the hole she'd gone through with John. Liv had responded that she hadn't liked going into the hole and that her new favorite color was pink. Though tempted to discover if she could communicate with her daughter telepathically, Celeste had decided to wait. Her baby had been through enough. Plus, she wanted to get Maxine's take on how to explain to Olivia when it was okay to go into the hole or talk with her mind.

For now, Celeste wanted to know about this secret Maxine and Ian shared.

"Would you like coffee?" Celeste asked Maxine again.

"I'm good, thank you." She looked to Ian. "How are you?"

"I think I'll be better after we get this conversation out of the way. It's been weighing on my mind."

Maxine nodded. "Mine, too." When she met Celeste's gaze, her eyes held apology. "I'm tired of carrying around this unwanted burden."

"It's a burden I forced on you," Ian said.

When Mason began to fuss, Celeste took him from Ian, then sat on the floor next to Olivia and the dog. "What's the burden?" she asked, settling her son on the area rug. Ever since John had mentioned the secret, she'd tried coming up with what they could've been keeping from her that had to do with her mother. While she'd considered what Dr. Ryker had said about Maxine, there'd been no mention of her mentor in his case file. And if Maxine had known her mom, she would've told Celeste. They were too close, and she trusted her friend.

"It's amazing how much you take after Janice." Ian positioned himself at the edge of the recliner. "Not only in looks, or your gifts, but your attitude and strength. She was a strong, stubborn woman with a kind heart. Well, kind to everyone but me." He gave her a quick smile that didn't reach his eyes. "You know all about her kidnapping, and how I chose to send another team after her, rather than go myself."

"She never forgave you for that," Celeste said, remembering some of what her mom had written in her journal.

He cleared his throat. "Janice also wanted nothing to do with working for the FBI afterward. I couldn't blame her. I tried apologizing for my actions, but she wouldn't listen."

"I know all of this." When Celeste had first met Ian, he'd explained to her how he'd chosen his career over his daughter, and how he'd given up his parental rights to her, allowing her dad, Hugh, to adopt her. "I want to know why Olivia thinks both you and Maxine have a secret about my mother."

Ian released a deep breath. "I lied to you about why Janice refused to let me see you. Yes, she was still holding a grudge against me for not coming for her, but it was more than that. You see, I liked Ryker's super-spy idea, just not what he'd done to those people. I've worked with many psychics over the years, and believe they can be of great value during certain investigations. Your mother worried I liked the super-spy idea too much. Because she'd witnessed first-hand what Ryker had done to his victims, and because those victims were psychic or had special abilities, she was scared for you even before you were born. She didn't want you to end up like Karen Webber." Frowning, he shook his head. "I would have never used you in that way. Ever."

"But you've had no problem using Celeste on a couple CORE investigations," John reminded him.

"That's different. Working an investigation is one thing. Performing psychic-enhancing experiments on my own child would be deranged. For Janice to even have thought that I would have done anything to harm Celeste was ridiculous."

"There was nothing in my mother's journals about this," Celeste said, unsure if he was telling the truth.

"I told him," Maxine admitted.

This had to be a mistake. "You?" Celeste stared at Maxine, confusion and denial tearing through her stomach and twisting it into a knot. "How did you know?"

Maxine's forehead wrinkled with worry. "I knew Janice. I'm so sorry, dear. I should have told you."

"You think?" The betrayal stung, hurt badly. "I trusted you. How many times have I brought up my mother?" Celeste asked, her throat clogging with tears. "God, Maxine. Friday morning I told you I was hoping to connect with her, and to get answers. All along you could've given them to me."

"Celeste, stop and let me explain," Ian said. "I met Maxine years before I met Janice. When I started with the FBI and was working a difficult case, I would occasionally bring in Maxine as a psychic consultant. After I heard about Janice and her work with the Baltimore PD, I brought her onboard, too. I introduced Maxine to Janice, and from there the two became friends."

"We were very close." Maxine's lips curled into a wistful smile. "We were intrigued by each other's different abilities and would get together and have psychic sessions, much like what you and I do."

Celeste was too angry to return the smile. "In other words, you knew the extent of my mother's gift." When Maxine nodded, the hurt cut deeper. "Here I've been struggling with my abilities, and you could've simply told me what I needed to know."

"I wanted to tell you the truth." A tear slipped down Maxine's cheek. "But Ian and I both felt it was best for you to learn about your gift on your own."

"Neither of you had any right to decide what was best for Celeste," John said with irritation. "None."

"That's right," Celeste added, her voice rising as the anger surfaced. "You could've at least told me you and Mom were friends."

"If Maxine had, you would've pushed her to tell you everything." Ian stood. "For two years you'd repressed your gift. When it came back, your ability to see the dead and the past was stronger than ever. If Maxine had told you about the other things you could possibly do, things your mother had done, it would've been too overwhelming." He walked to the built-in bookshelves and picked up the photograph of Celeste and her mother. "By not teaching you the extent of your gift, your mother did you a disservice."

"Don't say that." Maxine also stood. "Janice was trying to protect her daughter."

"How would you know?" He set down the photo. "And why are you defending her? She cut you out of her life, too."

"No, she didn't. We stayed in contact until she died." Maxine turned away from Ian and faced Celeste. "Your mom loved you so much, all she ever wanted was for you to have a normal life. She didn't look at her abilities as a gift, but more of a dirty secret. When she realized you were just like her, she tried to stifle what you could do."

"Why?" Celeste asked.

"She'd claimed her gift was bigger than her, and that she had no right to own it." Maxine went to Celeste, then sat next to her. She took her hand. "Celeste, Ian's right. You're so much like your mother, but unlike Janice, you've embraced who you are, even during your moments of doubt. Janice never could. Instead of appreciating the blessing she'd been given, she eventually became scared of it. She couldn't stomach seeing the dead, or watching what victims had gone through just before they'd died. After she found out she was pregnant with you, she told me she didn't want her children to have her abilities because if the wrong people knew, they could be hurt. But she also feared what her children might see." Maxine glanced to Olivia. "You can understand that, can't you? I've noticed you don't bring Olivia into my house anymore. Is it because she can see my ghosts?"

Celeste nodded. "I should've told you. I'm worried about her learning to distinguish the difference between the living and the dead. I should have told you."

Maxine gave her hand a squeeze. "We should have both been honest with each other. Please believe me, I held back my knowledge to help you, not hurt you. If I'd told you your mother could not only communicate with the dead, but that she was telepathic and could perform remote viewing in the present, I think it would have been too much to handle all at once. That's how it was for your mother. Your grandma told her what she was, when Janice was about seven or eight. Imagine what that must've been like for her. To be so young and immature, and yet to possess powers the average person doesn't believe exists. Then to be told to suppress it."

Celeste stared at Maxine. "Suppress it? My grandmother told my mom this?" Her grandma had passed away when Celeste was ten. All Celeste could remember about her was that she'd been sweet and loving, and could bake just about anything.

"Unfortunately. Your grandma didn't want people to know. From what I understand, your great-grandma used to give psychic readings from her basement. People from all around Maryland would come and see her." Maxine grinned. "Apparently your grandma hadn't wanted to follow in her mother's footsteps."

"If my grandma taught my mom to suppress her gift, how'd she end up working for the FBI?"

Maxine looked to Ian. "Do you remember the story?" she asked.

"I do," he said. "In the late '70s, Janice was renting a row house that'd been built in 1875. A woman had been killed two units down from Janice's. Police were unable to solve the crime, and the case went cold. Months later, the woman's ghost began haunting Janice, to the point where your mother launched her own investigation into her neighbor's past. By using her psychic ability, she was able to give the Baltimore PD information which led to a conviction. From there, a few Baltimore detectives kept contacting Janice and asking her for help. She was reluctant, but she had a big heart and couldn't turn her back on the ghosts who needed her."

"Sounds like someone else I know," Maxine said, her eyes shining with pride. "Darling, I'm sorry for not being honest with you. Not being able to talk to you about Janice has been utter torture for me. She was one of my closest friends. Losing her…" A tear slipped down her cheek. "I loved your mom. I love you, too. Can you forgive me? Losing you would destroy me."

Celeste adored Maxine, especially when she was melodramatic. Losing their friendship would destroy her, too. Could she move past the deceit? Were the lies and half-truths worth ending their relationship? More importantly, could she manage her way through the psychic world without Maxine?

She looked to John and drew in a fortifying breath when he gave her an encouraging nod. She glanced to her son, who'd pulled himself up into a crawl position and was rocking back and forth. Olivia was next to him, smiling and encouraging him to move.

Celeste had more growing to do, more to learn and so much to share with her children. She didn't want to do it alone. She wanted a friend by her side, someone who truly understood her gift. Someone who cared and loved her and her family.

Celeste hugged Maxine. "I love you, and I forgive you." She pulled back and met Maxine's watery gaze. "I get why you lied to me, but don't ever do it again."

Maxine pulled her in for another hug. "Never."

Celeste looked over Maxine's shoulder to Ian. The guilt saddening his face tugged at her heart. Her father had made many mistakes, and could possibly leave this world with too much regret hanging onto his soul. She didn't want that for him. Yes, he'd been selfish in his youth, and manipulative in his prime, but, deep down, he was a good man. And there was no doubt in her mind that he loved her and her family.

"Mason big boy," Olivia shouted, and clapped.

Celeste leaned back from Maxine to look at her son, who moved his arms and legs, and crawled for the first time.

"He sure is." Ian dropped to his knees. Grinning, he patted the area rug, encouraging Mason to keep crawling. "Come to Grandpa."

Tears stung Celeste's eyes as she shifted her gaze from Mason to Ian. And it hit her. Ian had never been able to experience this 'first' with her. Because he'd chosen his career over family, and because of her mother's fears and unwillingness to forgive him, Ian had missed out on so many firsts. Some people would probably think she was nuts for allowing the man into her life. After all, he'd given up his parental rights to her. Maybe she was crazy, or maybe life was just too damned short to stay bitter and angry.

While Mason put on a show, Olivia came over and sat on Celeste's lap. She took Maxine's hand. "Where Edwart?"

"He doesn't leave my house," Maxine said.

Olivia frowned. "Why?"

"Because that's where he lives," Celeste replied.

"Why?"

Hoping to distract her daughter from a marathon of 'why' questions, Celeste tickled Olivia. Liv laughed and pushed off her lap to crawl around with Mason.

"I think Olivia's going to need serious mentoring," Celeste said. "She doesn't know the difference between ghosts and living people. That's a problem."

"It certainly is," Maxine concurred. "Then there's her telepathic ability, and yours. Have you discovered your gift?"

Celeste noticed Ian's attention was now on her. "I have. But it's not something I think I want."

"Unfortunately, you're stuck with it," Maxine said. "Not to worry. Your mother explained how it worked for her, and how she could turn it off or on at any given time."

"Good to know, and hopefully we'll be able to teach Olivia this. I don't want her planting what she wants for Christmas in my head," she said, thinking of the story Karen told her.

Maxine and Ian stayed for a little while. Instead of discussing Ryker or psychic abilities, they talked about the dog Cami wanted to adopt, the summer party Maxine planned to host in a few weeks, and laughed at Mason as he showed off his new crawling skills.

As they were leaving, Ian hesitated at the door. "I hope you understand why I wasn't honest with you about Maxine and

Janice."

"I do, and I'll get over it. Just promise you won't lie to me again."

"I promise." He embraced her. "I used to look at CORE and my other business investments as my legacy," he said, releasing her. "I was wrong. You and my grandkids are. Thank you for allowing me to be a part of your lives."

With tears moistening her eyes and clogging her throat, she couldn't respond. She kissed his cheek, then stood in the doorway and watched him go. John came to the doorway carrying Mason. Olivia squeezed between their legs, and once she was on the front porch, she waved and yelled good-bye to Ian and Maxine.

After their cars had disappeared around the corner, Celeste looked to John. "It's beautiful outside and we've got the whole day ahead of us. What do you want to do?" she asked him.

"Go park an play."

Celeste and John glance to Olivia, who covered her mouth and giggled.

"You heard her?" he whispered.

"Yep."

"When are you going to start taking Liv to your psychic sessions?"

She blew out a breath. "Apparently not soon enough."

John chuckled and looked to Olivia. "Hey, Daddy's got a great idea. Why don't we have a picnic at the park?" After Olivia rushed past them and into the house, saying she needed her shoes, John lifted Mason until they were nose to nose. "Don't get any ideas from your sister. I don't want your baby babble in my head," he said, then turned to her. "We're in so much trouble."

"At least life won't be boring."

He wrapped an arm around her as they headed into the house to pack for the park. "Are you doing okay? Maxine and Ian laid a lot on you."

"Honestly, I'm good. I still have plenty of questions for Maxine about my mom, but at least I'll have her to help me muddle through all of this."

"And your dad?"

"Ian? I'm not mad at him. Being upfront isn't his style. I would like to see the files he has on us. You know, the ones Vigo saw."

"Ask to see them," John suggested. "If he tells you no, then scare the hell out of him by throwing things around the room with your mind."

Celeste grinned. "I'm sure that'd go over well. You're right, though. It wouldn't hurt to ask." Once they were in the kitchen, and she'd started packing their lunches, she asked John what his plans were for the rest of the week.

"I'm still on vacation, remember?"

"Right. Some vacation," she said, and decided to approach him with her plan. "Since you're still off work, would you want to take a road trip? No kids. Eden offered to take them overnight."

"Are we sleeping in the car? Because I'm not sure I can handle staying at a hotel yet."

"Oh, stop. It'll be fine. It's about a nine-hour drive. We'll stay the night, then head home in the morning."

John sat Mason on the floor. "Sounds like a lot of driving to turn around and come right home. What's the destination?"

"Federal Correctional Institution, Cumberland, Maryland."

Three days later...
Federal Correctional Institution, Cumberland, Maryland
Friday, 4:44 p.m. Eastern Daylight Time

CELESTE SAT ON the chair located in front of the glass partition of the non-contact prison visiting room. Seconds later, the door opened and Dr. Seth Ryker stepped inside, then took a seat. God, she hated the man. Beyond despicable, redemption or remorse, he didn't deserve to live, not when he was responsible for so many deaths.

Never taking his gaze from her, he lifted the receiver from the phone on the wall. "You look just like your mother."

"So I've been told."

"I'm not surprised you would come here." His face stony, he studied her. "Are you nervous?" he asked, superiority in his tone.

She'd been cool and collected during the days leading up to the road trip to Cumberland, Maryland, and had spent that time enjoying Chicago's touristy activities with her family. But family time hadn't been the only thing that had kept her relaxed and happy. Since leaving the Rykers', then talking with Maxine and Ian, she'd never been more self-aware. Her mother had mistaken her gift as a burden. Celeste would never judge her mother for believing that, but it saddened her, because there were victims—invisible to the majority of the world—walking amongst them, and seeking justice. Helping those people was a beautiful thing. A gift. A blessing. Facing the arrogant man who'd murdered the people she had helped free was a wonderful, vengeful bonus.

"Not at all," she said, bringing the memories of what he'd done to Karen to the forefront of her mind.

"You're facing your mother's past. Let's not forget that my mother and son had kidnapped you."

"Let's also not forget your son is dead and your mother will die in prison," she countered.

His conceit momentarily slipped, and she relished the pain in his eyes. Based on the reading she'd performed on Aiden, she gathered that Dr. Ryker genuinely cared for his son. Now the man knew what it was like to suffer right alongside the families of his victims.

"Does it make you feel good to know my son is dead?" he asked, his tone clinical, as if he were her psychiatrist rather than a convicted killer.

"Honestly, no. I'm not sorry he's dead, but I don't think his death was necessary. I think Martha manipulated Aiden. Do you have any idea how evil she is, how cruel? You must, since you told her you wished she'd die."

He blinked a few times. "What are you talking about?"

"I did a reading on Aiden and witnessed your conversation with him and Martha. You know the one where they told you in detail how they planned to kidnap and make me their test subject."

"Amazing. What are your other psychic abilities?"

"Your son is dead and that's what you want to know?" Celeste gripped the handset. "Clearly thirty-five years in prison hasn't changed you."

"I apologize. That was crass. But you have to understand, prison hasn't changed my fascination with the psychic phenomena. As for wanting my mother dead..." Anger flashed in his eyes. "She killed my wife."

"I know. I saw her do it." Celeste said, surprised Ryker was aware of Sally's murder.

"In the coal room." He leaned forward. His brow deepened into an angry V. "Had Sally lived, I don't believe I would be sitting across from you today. I loved my wife. When my head got too high in the clouds, she would bring me back to solid ground. Losing her devastated me. During that time when I thought she'd left me to start a new life, the government and military were also rejecting my theories and boiling them down to nothing but nonsensical science fiction. I was so damned determined to prove them wrong, and I needed something positive in my life."

"I can see how killing five people would be a positive thing," she said with heavy sarcasm.

He showed no regret, not even a brief spark of remorse. Instead, he half shrugged. "Had I been given more time, I could've proven my theories correct."

"Or killed more people. Why didn't you tell the police Martha had murdered Sally?"

"I didn't know until ten years into my sentence. My mother came to see me and confessed to doing it. She'd said Sally's body was buried in the mass grave at Forest Haven. But so are hundreds of others. What evidence could I offer to police? Even if they'd found Sally's remains, I'm quite sure the police would've pinned her murder on me. They could have said my motivation was to get Sally out of the way so I had the opportunity to run my experiments."

He had a valid point. "Did Martha say why she killed Sally?"

"Because she was in the way. Once Sally was gone, she pushed and encouraged me to move forward with my research, and even helped me prepare the house for my patients. I've had many years to consider what happened during that time. I believe my mother set me up to fail, especially because I'm fairly certain she was the one who made the anonymous call that led to my arrest."

"Why do you think she wanted you to fail?" she asked, certain he was, once again, correct. Martha enjoyed inflicting pain and being in control. The moment Dr. Ryker had brought his first subject into their house, he'd given his mother the opportunity to continue where she'd left off after retiring from Forest Haven.

"Money, and Aiden. I'd made the mistake of telling her that if my research was a success, Aiden and I would likely move wherever the government sent us. She'd miss the money and her grandson."

"The one she murdered."

Dr. Ryker looked away. "I…don't understand why she did it." When he faced her again, tears misted his eyes. "Aiden thought I looked at him as a disappointment. He'd been so wrong. I loved my son. I wasn't a good father, but I loved him."

Celeste tried to muster an ounce of empathy for the man, but failed. "Then you should have stopped him and Martha. Because you didn't, Aiden and George Meadows are dead, and I could've been killed if I hadn't escaped."

"Tell me, do you know how George Meadows died?" Ryker asked, rather than admitting he was at fault. "My mother's attorney came to see me. He's hoping I'll testify that she's in the early phases of Alzheimer's in order to keep her out of prison and, instead, get her placed in a secured nursing home." He let out a breath. "After I refused, he wouldn't tell me anything about what my mother and Aiden had done."

Not about to give the man the satisfaction of knowing his theory had been somewhat proven, she shook her head.

"Can you tell me what types of experiments they performed on you?"

The man was sick. "Why? So you can lie in bed fantasizing about it?"

Dr. Ryker cleared his throat. "Of course not."

"Look, I didn't come here to ask why you did what you did thirty-five years ago, or how you feel about your mother. I don't care about your feelings or your motivations. I care about justice."

"I'm doing my time, and my mother will, too."

"That's not good enough. Not for me. You're not sorry for what you've done, you're sorry you were caught. I shouldn't be surprised that you want to know what they did to me and George, but I am. Your son is dead. Your own mother slit his throat. If I were in your position, I wouldn't want to talk to me. I'd be too busy grieving. But your ego, your belief in your theories, and your fascination with people like me couldn't keep you away."

"I loved my son," he repeated.

"And it's your fault he's dead. If you had told the authorities Aiden and Martha's plans, he'd still be alive, and so would George. Everything that happened now and thirty-five years ago was your fault. You chose to perform unethical and inhumane experiments, and you chose to allow your son to do the same." She glanced at one of the prison guards, before meeting Dr. Ryker's gaze. "Do you ever think about Karen Webber?"

While his face remained grim, his eyes shined with excitement. "Yes. It was unfortunate she didn't survive. Karen was *very* special."

"I know. She's the reason I came here today. Karen was with me the entire time I was being held in your basement. She...*showed* me things, and taught me about myself. Before I go, would you like to see what I learned?"

Ryker gripped the receiver tightly, his knuckles growing white. "Yes." His Adam's apple bobbed as he swallowed hard. "Please show me."

Celeste placed herself back in the Rykers' basement. Watched as the police and FBI kicked in the door of the room where she was being held. She then stepped into the room and stared at Martha, bloodied and holding the scalpel. She froze the image, and concentrated on Dr. Ryker.

"Do you see it?" she asked, hoping she'd planted the gruesome picture inside his head.

His face crumpled with misery and grief. Tears filled his eyes. "My God," he whispered, his gaze widening with horror. "How could she?"

"Did you know?" Celeste asked.

He shook his head, blinked, then looked at her. "I had no idea. They didn't tell me how he'd died, just that it happened and that she did it." He released a quiet sob. "There's so much blood…on him, on her hands."

"On yours, too. Good-bye, Dr. Ryker."

Celeste pulled the handset away from her ear. Before she hung it up, she stopped, released it, then used her mind to hold it in the air. Dr. Ryker glanced from the receiver to her, and back to the receiver again, just as she set it in the phone's cradle. While Dr. Ryker gaped at her, and more tears streamed down his face, she stood and smiled, then she gave him the finger.

She left the visiting room and met up with John in the hallway. "Are you okay?" he asked, once they'd signed out and were leaving the building.

"I'm great. It's weird. I feel like a huge weight has been lifted from me."

"You showed him Aiden and Martha?"

She nodded. "He saw it," she said, then told him how Dr. Ryker had reacted, and what they'd discussed. "He can never be released from prison. There's no remorse there, and I think he still has an obsession with psychics. Oh, and I gave him the finger."

John chuckled and opened her car door. "The other day Olivia flipped off Mason when he tried to take her Vlad. Now I know where she learned that little trick."

"Really?" Crap. She needed to have more self-control, but the middle finger was a simple gesture that said so much. "I'll try to refrain when the kids are in the car." She looked toward the prison. "I showed him something no parent should ever have to see. Why don't I feel an ounce of guilt?"

"Why should you? Ryker isn't going to be held accountable for what Martha and Aiden did. Agent Dickenson said Martha claimed Ryker knew, but there's no proof."

"I wish they'd been able to find the letter from Vigo."

"Even if they had, what then? Ryker is never going to be free. Which is why I like your brand of justice. Now he can spend the rest of his life with the image of his mother killing his son stuck in his head." He touched her cheek, drawing her attention away from the prison. "It's over. The Rykers aren't worth another thought."

"You're right. They're not. Come on, let's go." Once they were in the car and John was driving toward the exit, she said, "There is *one* more thing I need to do."

"Let me take you out for a nice dinner, then go back to the hotel for hours of uninterrupted sex?"

She grinned. "You read my mind."

Chuckling, he shook his head. "Liar."

"No. Marathon sex is top priority. But when we get home tomorrow, I think I'll stop by Ian's."

"For?"

"I want the files he has on us. I promised Olivia we'd roast marshmallows tomorrow night, and we could use some paper to get our fire started."

John grinned. "You know how much I love you, right?"

She did. She also knew she couldn't live without him, and just like John, she would do anything to protect her family. Even go up against her father.

She took his hand and squeezed. "As much as I love you."

EPILOGUE

The next evening...
Ian and Cami's house, Chicago, Illinois
Saturday, 5:47 p.m. Central Daylight Time

"THEN I GAVE him the finger and left."

Ian Scott looked away from his daughter, stood, then went to the mini-bar tucked in the office bookcase. "Would you like a drink?" He sure as hell needed one. If he'd known Celeste planned to pay Dr. Seth Ryker a visit, he would have called the prison warden and prevented it. He didn't care that Ryker couldn't get to her. After all the man had done, after what his mother and son had tried to do, he just didn't want Celeste anywhere near the man.

He poured two fingers of scotch. Considering what Celeste had just told him, and what he would have to inform her of, he added another finger's worth.

"I could use something strong," she said. "But don't kill me. I promised Liv we'd have a fire tonight. You know how she loves s'mores. You and Cami should come by and join us. Eden and Hudson will be there. My brother and Lloyd will, too. Dante and Jessica might stop by with the kids."

"Sounds like a night with the family," he said, making her a vodka tonic.

"Which you are."

"I'll talk to Cami about it," he said, handing her the drink.

"I might've already mentioned it to her. And she may or may not be gathering up things to bring."

Ian couldn't stop the smile tugging at his mouth. His fiancée loved impromptu parties. Even more, she adored Celeste's family. "Why doesn't this surprise me?"

She took a sip of her drink. "So...no comment about my visit with Ryker?"

He sat next to her on the leather couch. "What Ryker had to say about his mother was interesting. It almost sounds as if she'd planned everything. She took his idea of performing human experiments, and made it a reality, starting with murdering Sally Ryker. I also believe Ryker is probably right about his wife. Even if the police find her body, other than what you viewed during your reading—which is inadmissible—there's no evidence or witnesses investigators could use against Martha."

"After what she did to his son, I think Dr. Ryker will be willing to tell the police what he knows."

He shook his head. "I think you need to let this go. Martha confessed to kidnapping and assaulting you and George Meadows, taking part in the surgery that led to Meadows' death and killing Aiden. I was told her attorney is trying to work out a plea agreement with the state's attorney."

"She wants to live in a nursing home and claims she has Alzheimer's," Celeste said with an eye roll. "That woman knew exactly what she was doing, and is as sharp as the scalpel she'd used on Aiden."

Ian half smiled. "Everyone involved in the case agrees. It's possible Martha could be placed in a prison hospital, but I think that will only happen if she gives them something more."

"Like confessing to fifty-nine other murders?" Celeste shook her head. "I wish I was able to get in her head and understand why she did it."

"You don't believe her 'because I can' excuse?"

"Do you?"

"I do." He leaned into the cushion. "I've met plenty of murderers over the years. During investigations we always look for motive. Sometimes there just aren't any, as if they were born bad and without a conscience. I think Martha is one of those people." He took another drink. "When you were at the prison, did you get inside Ryker's head?"

When Celeste faced him, her eyes held suspicion. "I don't want to discuss that part of my gift. I want Maxine to teach me how to control it, so I can help Olivia in the future. Then I want to forget I possess it. Please don't get any ideas of using me to help with your investigations."

Damn, he still had a way to go to earn his daughter's complete trust. "That's not why I asked," he replied honestly. Although he would like to use Celeste's new ability to CORE's advantage, he loved his daughter and, unless she could teach herself how to unsee images or erase her memories, he didn't want her entering the minds of killers. He released a deep breath. "Celeste, Ryker was found dead in his cell this morning. He hanged himself."

She held his gaze, brought the glass to her lips, then took several long swallows. "Darla was right."

"Darla Kemper?"

She set the empty glass on the table. "Before I left the Rykers', she told me she'd predicted Aiden would die young and violently, and Seth would die by his own hand." Frowning, she looked to her lap. "I did plant an image in his head."

"What was it?"

"Martha, right after she'd slit Aiden's throat." She looked at him and cocked a brow. "I guess it was more than he could handle."

"Don't feel any guilt over this," he said, taking her hand.

"Who said I did? He could've stopped Martha and Aiden, and didn't. So I showed him his mother for who she really is, and the end result of his poor choices." She squeezed his hand, released it, then stood. "Have you heard how Martha has reacted to her son's death?"

"No, but if I do, I'll let you know."

"Please don't. Unless you're telling me she's dead, I don't want to waste my time or energy on her." She glanced to the wall where the painting of Chicago's skyline hung, and also hid his built-in safe. "Before I leave, I'd like the files you have on me, John and Olivia. I'm assuming you don't have one on Mason, but if you do, I'd like that, too."

Guilt followed him as he rose, then walked toward the painting. "When I discovered Vigo had gone through my files, I moved certain documents here."

"John suggested as much." She walked toward him. "Why have them in the first place? I can understand having files on me and John, but Olivia?"

He slid the painting aside, then began unlocking the safe. "They were for me. I never planned to share them."

"Again, why have them in the first place?"

He opened the safe, then withdrew four manila folders. "Rachel has taught me that computers are too vulnerable to hackers, which is why I prefer paper files over electronic." He turned to her. "I didn't create files on you and your family with malicious intent. I have files on everyone. Even Cami." He nodded to the large file cabinet near his desk. "There are hundreds in there, in the closet, and at my CORE office. You should see the banker's boxes I have in the basement."

She grinned. "You're a file hoarder?"

"I am," he admitted. Even as a kid he would write down events, then file them away in his bedroom closet. He didn't know how or why the habit had started, just that he had a compulsion to jot down everything. "In my defense, file hoarding has come in handy numerous times. Past investigations, information on people, places and events have helped me solve many unrelated cases."

"I can see that," she said, taking the files from him. "There're are four here. So you did have one on Mason."

"No, the fourth is your mother's. It's one that's separate from the original Ryker case. You know the majority of the information in there. If you don't want it, I can put it back in the safe."

"No, I'll keep it." She shoved the folders into her over-sized purse. "Thanks...Dad."

Warmth spread through him as he stared at his daughter. "I haven't been much of a father. No matter how hard I try, I'll never be anything like Hugh. He's a good man, and did a beautiful job raising you."

She stepped closer. "This isn't a competition of who's the better dad. I'm grateful Hugh adopted me and loved me as his own. I'm also grateful to have you in my life. I have two dads who love me. How lucky am I?" She kissed his cheek, then hugged him. "I don't always know what to do with you, but I do know *you're* a good man who would do anything for me and my family. I'd say that makes you a great father."

He hugged her back. "I'm a work in progress."

Chuckling, she stepped back. "Aren't we all? Since everyone is coming by soon, I better get going. I'll see you in a bit."

"Before you go, I know you don't want to discuss the Rykers, but there's one thing that's been bothering me."

She stopped in the doorway. "What's that?"

"How did you get out of the restraints? You told the FBI you ripped through them after Aiden started cutting you, but how? Why then and not before?"

"I did try before my *surgery*. I must've loosened the threads, so when I freaked out over being cut, they tore."

"Your medical report indicated no bruising along the places where you were restrained."

"I don't bruise easily," she said, her expression puzzled. "What's with the questioning? Is there an answer you're expecting me to give?"

Based on the broken light, the overturned cabinet and cart, along with the torn restraints, he hadn't been sure what to think. "Karen Webber was telepathic and telekinetic. You communicated with her ghost. Was it possible she helped you escape?"

"I've thought about it, but I'm not sure. Everything happened so quickly, and my head was face down at the time. All that matters is that I got free."

"Of course," he said, not believing her. Her answer was too

convenient and flippant.

"You don't look convinced." She grinned. "Were you waiting for me to tell you *I* destroyed the room with my mind?"

"No, honey. I'm sorry. You know me. I have a hard time taking a break from being an investigator. Get home. Cami and I will see you soon."

"Looking forward to it," she said, then left the room, leaving the door open.

Seconds later, the office door moved on its hinges and clicked shut. The hair along Ian's arms rose. He rushed to the door, opened it, then stepped onto the interior balcony overlooking his foyer, just as Celeste reached the bottom step. As the foyer door opened on its own, she looked up at him. Then, with a wink and a wave, she left.

I'll be damned. Ian chuckled and shook his head.

His daughter was a total badass.

✧ ✧ ✧

Kristine will raffle off one $50 gift card among all subscribers of her newsletter each month. To sign up for Kristine's email newsletter and for more information about her books go to www.kristinemason.net.

Celeste and her family need a vacation.

After a well-deserved rest, they'll be back!

Other Books by Kristine Mason

Psychic C.O.R.E. Series

Celeste Files: Unlocked (Book 1)

Some secrets should remain locked in the past...

Celeste Kain hasn't had a psychic vision in two years. After being brutally attacked while helping criminal investigation agency CORE stop a serial killer, her mind repressed her clairvoyant abilities. Married to CORE agent, John Kain, mother to their toddler, Olivia, and owner of an up-and-coming bakery, Celeste has been doing fine psychic-free. Only now the dead are using her body to tell their stories again...putting her new life and family at risk.

Haunted by a murdered woman, Celeste turns to a psychic mentor to learn how to control her gift, protect her family and bring justice to the dead. But the more she digs into the dead woman's past, the further she slips into the unknown, unlocking secrets literally worth killing for. As the body count rises, it becomes clear: someone in the dead woman's family is deeply, violently *wrong*. And Celeste needs to be careful, before she loses something more precious to her than her life.

Celeste Risinski, the heroine of Shadow of Danger (Book 1 C.O.R.E. Shadow Trilogy), is back with her own series. Join her as she learns how to deal with being a wife, mom, baker and...psychic investigator.

Celeste Files: Unjust (Book 2)

Dealing with the dead is murder...

Psychic Celeste Kain has two things on her mind, relaxing for a week in Florida with her husband, John, and making a baby. But a fishing trip turns her vacation into a nightmare when she reels in the body of a dead boat captain and accidentally unleashes an evil ghost who has one thing on his mind...revenge.

As the dead boat captain haunts Celeste, she looks deeper into his past and discovers that his murderer had done the world a favor. The ghost tormenting Celeste doesn't see it that way and will go to any length to avenge his death. If Celeste won't give him what he wants, he will take over her body and use her as a weapon...to kill her husband.

Celeste Files: Unforgotten (Book 3)

Something is wrong with the children...

Seven years ago, CORE agent, Dante Russo and his wife, Jessica, faced a parent's ultimate fear...their ten-month-old daughter was abducted. With no clues, not a single sighting or trace of evidence to keep hope alive, the case went cold...until now.

When the ghosts of murdered children begin to haunt psychic Celeste Kain, she's forced to get involved in her most challenging case yet. The ghosts know who has Sophia. They know her kidnapper intimately. They know him as Daddy, and as their killer.

Using psychic visions and the clues the young spirits provide, Celeste and her husband, John, travel across the country, desperately searching for the girl and her kidnapper. The dead children have made their warning clear...find Sophia before Daddy kills again.

Celeste Files: Poisoned (Book 4)

The walls are infected, the foundation is diseased...this house is poisoned.

CORE agent, Hudson Patterson and his wife, Eden, recently moved into a century-old mini-mansion. But their dream home has become a living nightmare—occupied by a malevolent spirit who will only share the residence with them and their daughter...in exchange for their souls.

Psychic Celeste Kain is four weeks away from giving birth. The last thing she wants to deal with is the dead. But when she realizes an evil presence is terrorizing Eden, she will go to any length to help her sister. Especially when she discovers there isn't just one ghost in Eden's house, but many other tortured souls trapped within its infected walls.

To put an end to the haunting, Celeste uses her unique gift to connect with the ghostly residents. But the wicked entity who has been feeding off the other spirits' pain and misery has other plans. It wants Celeste and her unborn child, and imprisons her inside the ghost house. Now powerless, unable to free herself and in labor, Celeste needs to fight to find her way back to her body before the entity can take what it wants...her baby.

Celeste Files: Possessed (Book 5)

Her husband is a killer...

John Kain is possessed, trapped in his own body while an evil spirit takes over his life. But the sinister ghost isn't just interested in a second chance at life. He has a diabolical agenda, one that involves murdering John's family.

Months ago, psychic Celeste Kain sent the dead 1920s gangster,

Vigo Donati, to Hell. Or so she thought... When her husband becomes erratic, violent and out of control, she finds a hidden cache of prescription drugs and worries John has an addiction. Until a psychic vision shows Vigo killing a man. The coincidence is too much and she's convinced the gangster has taken control of John.

With her family in danger and John's life at stake, Celeste needs to rid her husband of Vigo's spirit before he uses John's body to kill. Because if Vigo wins, she'll lose John forever...

C.O.R.E. Shadow Trilogy

Shadow of Danger (Book 1)
Shadow of Perception (Book 2)
Shadow of Vengeance (Book 3)

Ultimate C.O.R.E. Trilogy

Ultimate Kill (Book 1)
Ultimate Fear (Book 2)
Ultimate Prey (Book 3)

C.O.R.E. Above the Law

Perfectly Twisted (Book 1)
Perfectly Toxic (Book 2)
Perfectly Tortured (Book 3)

Sinful C.O.R.E.

Sinful Deeds (Book 1)

About Kristine Mason

Kristine Mason is the bestselling author of the popular romantic suspense trilogies, C.O.R.E. Shadow and Ultimate C.O.R.E. and C.O.R.E. Above the Law. She is currently working on her next C.O.R.E. series, along with more Psychic C.O.R.E. novels.

Although Kristine has published a few contemporary romance novels, she focuses most of her energy on her romantic suspense stories, which she loves for their blend of dark mystery/suspense and sexy romance. She is fascinated with what makes people afraid, and is famous for her depraved villains whose crimes present massive obstacles for her heroes and heroines to overcome.

Kristine has a degree in journalism from The Ohio State University and lives in Northeast Ohio with her husband, four kids, and adorable mutt. If she's not writing, she's chauffeuring kids, gardening, or collecting gnomes. Oh, and she makes a mean chocolate chip cookie, too!

Connect with Kristine on Facebook facebook.com/kristinemasonauthor, Twitter twitter.com/KristineMason7 or email her at authorkristinemason@gmail.com. You can also find out more about Kristine's books at www.kristinemason.net.

Printed in Great Britain
by Amazon